Letters from
The Lanai

Letters from The Lanai

By
Maili Yardley

Editions Limited

Copyright 2002 By Maili Yardley

Designed by Turner & de Vries, Ltd.
First Printing November 2002
123456789

Softcover
ISBN: 0-915013-22-3

Editions Limited
P.O. Box 10150
Honolulu, HI 96816
Telephone: (808) 735-7644
Facsimile: (808) 732-2164
E-mail: editionslimited@hawaii.rr.com

Printed in USA

This book is fondly dedicated to my grandchildren
Mikiala, Jonah, and Cynthia
whose letters I've cherished throughout the years

CONTENTS

Buzz Farnham 1916 - 1952

By Red McCoy

Sports lovers in the Islands mourn the passing of Dr. Walter "Buzz" Farnham yesterday from cancer at the age of 36.

Up until his recent illness, Farnham had been the doctor for the Kamehameha School football team. Reached on the Big Island, Henry Lindsay, outstanding quarterback on the Kam team, remembers when he suffered a serious spinal injury. Farnham was on the field in seconds and rode in the ambulance with him to Queen's Emergency Room. "If it hadn't been for his keeping in touch and constant encouragement, I might have given up in sheer discouragement. He was a real compassionate guy," Lindsay added.

"We lost a great volunteer coach of the University's swim team," said Larry Sakamoto, Director of Athletics at the University of Hawaii. "He was at the pool every Friday night during the season training the boys and working on their strokes and breathing. He introduced the game of water polo in which the Rainbows excelled and won many interscholastic games. Buzz was a stickler for good sportsmanship."

In prep school and college Farnham starred in football, was the captain of the swimming team and a champion pole vaulter.

This reporter can remember back in the mid '30s when competing polo teams played at Kapiolani Park. Farnham was the star of the Oahu Blues when he rode off the Maui player to make the long shot that broke the tie in the last second of the final chucker. Cars parked around the playing field blasted their horns and the crowds in the covered grandstand went wild with excitement.

Buzz Farnham played the game of life as a true sportsman.

Our aloha to his mother, Laura Farnham, and his sister, Prudence Farnham.

CHAPTER I

150 E 73rd St.
New York
February 23, 1952

Dear Prudence:

Since your wire informing me of Buzz's passing and the planned services arrived, I've been barely going through the motions of living. Wrote your mother earlier this evening and still feel I haven't said all I wanted to say. It's almost midnight and have just mixed myself another nightcap. Lucy is long since asleep, but tonight that won't come easily for me. I can't seem to face the fact Buzz has gone out of my life. My mind is awash with poignant memories of a super guy and staunch friend, and it is hard for me to comprehend what cancer could do that football, polo, crazy college driving, two days on a lousy raft in the Pacific, and wine, women, and song never could do!

Strange you and I never really knew one another after all these years, and yet how natural that I should turn to you now. You always seemed so much younger. How he loved you. He adored you. And so I loved the things he loved. He always referred to you as the "kid." Yes, you were a special person, and he was a very doting brother.

At prep school he was known as the "kid from Hawaii," and threw himself into football that first fall. Those barefoot kicks were sensational.

I remember those mornings at chapel when he and I had to light the candles and assist Father John... acolytes complete with the long white robes. At 15 we thought of ourselves as men! To prove it we conned some dago wine off of Charlie, the old gardener. But later your brother "blew it" out the dormer window. Unfortunately, it was snowing in Connecticut at the time.

College was another thing. We both zeroed in on the University of Pennsylvania, and the bond of friendship became firmer...the old Zete grip, brotherly love, and all that jazz. In those days it took weeks to travel back and forth to the Islands...four days overland by train and five or six days by steamer across the Pacific, then if connections were good an overnight boat ride to Kauai... as I remember, a very rough trip. So naturally your brother became a member of our family in Philadelphia during the holidays. Buzz never let on how homesick he was, but I could tell! Those main line debs weren't the same as the warm Island girls. But he was brave...he went along with Mrs. Shaw's formalities. My mother always said he just had to come from an outstanding family. She admired his honesty, manners, small considerations, and his bread and butter letters were always a signal that we kids were going to be taught a lesson in manners.

When we finally decided on our futures, I so well remember his turning to me and saying, "Pete, you tend to the heels and I'll do the healing." And if it weren't for some important heel in the middle of this big court case I would have been right there at the funeral with you today. Actually, with the five-hour time difference you have maybe just returned from the graveside services and I can picture you all sitting quietly on that spacious lanai overlooking the green hillsides slashed with red dirt and down to the blue ocean far below. My heart is with you all, believe me! I have lost more than a friend, dear Prudence.

You know, I haven't been on that lanai since the war ended. Heaven knows I slept, sat, played, and sang on it often enough, but not as much as we'd like to have. Being on Kauai with the Farnham family was like coming home and living a heaven on earth. Does that gem, Fusako, still wear the kimono? Having just returned from beating the Japanese, this never seemed to bother me. I guess it is always the individual.

I missed you then because you were a teenager away at boarding school in the East. Did you honestly hate it as much as you wrote Buzz? I shall never forget the day he received your letter. We got our mail that particular day just before going topside. He tore open your letter then smiled and said, "The 'kid' says it's awful back there...cold, has to wear shoes and she'd much rather be in blue jeans than those drab, sacky, itchy uniforms. So much for Foxcroft even though it has horses."

Then your picture fell out and I couldn't believe it was the same girl I remembered. Immediately, we hit the deck and were off on our missions, and I didn't see him again for months. Maybe I could compare the agony of not knowing his fate that night as knowing for sure tonight. If we hadn't heard of his rescue so soon, I was about to write you then. But you know the happy ending there. The Lord be praised. My last memory of Hawaii was that happy time on the lanai and my regret at leaving my old pal to continue his journey of healing. What a fine doctor he was, too, damn it, but no, I can't say not smart enough. He never married. I wonder now. When Lucy and I decided to get married, it was only natural that he fly East to be my best man. After all, Buzz had met Lucy when she came through Honolulu on her father's yacht after cruising around the world with her family, and it was really through him that Lucy and I eventually got together. I remember his writing me about this terrific blond with blue eyes who was such a good sport and loved being in Hawaii.

You were supposed to come to the wedding, but it was a summer garden affair on her grandmother's estate on Long Island, and you couldn't wait to get home from college to your horses. The pity, too, because it was a lovely wedding and your brother was so handsome in his cutaway. Again, all the girls flipped over that tanned blond from Hawaii. We left for our honeymoon. (Just fizzed myself another drink.) Now I mustn't imagine, no, but did he look at me in a strange way...did he overdo the old Zete grip? No, it must have been all that champagne. It certainly can't be all this Scotch! I don't think he even took advantage of the trip East to take a well-earned vacation but flew immediately home to all his devoted patients. What a guy! My heart aches for your mother. I know how much he meant to her, especially after your father died. Damn it...thirty-six is too darn young.

He and I always knew there was a God...we never really spoke of it at length, so to speak, but we went through some times when the old prep school chapel rote came in pretty handy and we gave thanks for this. I know in my heart that he is out of his misery and suffering in this transitory life...he saw so much of it...and he is with his heavenly Father. Come to think of it, he's probably looking down at me and saying, "For Pete's sake, ol' man, knock off and get to bed. The 'kid' will appreciate all this, but remember you've got a busy day tomorrow. Get some sleep so you can lick the h— out of those guys."

Maybe he's right, dear Prudence. Forgive me the rambling, but actually I feel so much better. Please let us keep in touch. So now if I can creep quietly to bed before our two-year-old wakes at the crack of dawn, I'll have it made. Count on me. Please let me be your big brother now.

Devotedly,
Pete Thorne

Kauai
March 9th, 1952

Dear Pete:

You'll never know how deeply appreciative I am to have your sympathetic letter. I treasure it. Knowing what devoted friends you and Buzz were, I knew it would be nostalgic, so I took it up to my room to open and read quietly. I shall always be grateful to you for sharing your memories. Mother especially appreciated your comforting letter to her and will write when she feels able. Naturally, Buzz's suffering and death has set her back considerably, but for 62 and at her point in life, she is doing remarkably well. She is happy to be back in her own home, and we are here on Kauai surrounded by the peace and beauty and faithful families of the ranch.

She sits on the lanai and reads the letters of sympathy that are coming from all over, but I can truthfully say that she has read and re-read your letter, so full of compassion, memories, and love. She smiles at your reference to visiting the apartment you and Buzz shared in that run- down, stately, fine old house in the city while attending college. Why she thought that her son would have a neat, respectable, and tastefully furnished apartment is beyond me...especially when he was brought up in a house of attentive domestics! She can laugh about it now. She's always considered you another son.

Everyone has been so solicitous and kind, and I can only say this to you...but why do people ask if there is anything they can do for you, and you think of a million things but politely say no? Are they assuaging their feelings by making the effort and thus relieved when you say no? It's funny, but the ranch hands' wives never ask...they just bring food they know will tempt us, do such small, kind things and offer to drive us here or there. Through our sorrows I have learned a lot. Pete, it is so good to be able to talk this way...people have been so kind and I do appreciate it.

After Papa died, Mama decided to move back to the ranch on Kauai so sold the Diamond Head house. Whenever we went to Honolulu, we stayed at the Halekulani Hotel, a favorite of kamaaina, owned by Mama's friends the Kimballs. That's where we were the last few weeks of Buzz's illness. Mrs. Kimball was so considerate and caring for Mama's welfare as the days at the hospital were very tiring for Mama. Naturally, she wouldn't have it any other way. He was so brave and cheerful but very thin and wan. When Mama and I would leave, I'd turn to give him a thumbs-up wave, and he'd press his thumb and forefinger between his lips and push as hard as he could. I got the message. He knew us up to the end and just sort of fell asleep holding Mama's hand. I thought I was prepared for this, but when the nurse took Mama's hand and nodded to me, I found I wasn't all that brave. Actually, I think I expected him to get up, put his arms around me and whisper, "It's all right, 'kid,' I'm here."

We didn't leave him immediately, and the nurses were so dear and patient, having worked with Buzz in the past. Mama called the bishop to ask him to please come and say the final prayers. Then we clung to one another sobbing, trying all the while to be brave for the others' sake. The bishop was there in minutes, and his comforting words and healing hands seemed to ease the pain and leave us with a certain peace. I think we both felt renewed in faith and courage to face the days ahead.

The bishop conducted the services at St. Andrew's Cathedral, which was filled to capacity...so they tell me. Since the bishop had known Buzz since he was a child, his delivery was very warm and meaningful, and short, in deference to Mama. Afterwards, we sat while people came to offer condolences, then Kua and his wife, Hattie, as well as Sara, the bishop, Mama, and I flew to Kauai and drove to the old graveyard on the ranch. It was a clear, sunny afternoon. I can remember the scent of lei and flowers filling the air with their strong perfume and yet I can't remember a face from that sea of people. The old ranch hands, generations of loyal Hawaiians, Japanese, Portuguese, and hapa, came, hats in hand, and a group of cowboys sang a few of Buzz's old Hawaiian favorites acapella. It was sad, but a great tribute to someone they all loved.

As the bishop began, "Death is a horizon," I gazed down the mountain out to sea and thought to myself..."No, you're not in that little bronze urn...you're out there, you're here, and you'll never leave us. What was it you used to love to say while we were swimming? Oh, yes, the 104th psalm — "who layeth the beams of his chambers in the waters" — and then you'd splash me and say, "think of God as the ocean and us as His waves, so we are one." I looked up and the bishop was waiting to speak to me, but I was still with Buzz, and he was still around me. I shall return many times to lay flowers there, but in my heart I know this is only a gesture of temporal remembrance.

Yes, we were on the lanai, just family and a few old

friends that evening. I felt so sorry for Sara. I know how much she loved him, too, and wonder if he had told her anything or just went along, using his practice as an excuse for not proposing. I wonder.

You were on the lanai, too, if only in spirit. It was an evening full of love and fond remembrances. While we were sitting there lost in thought with the last rays of the setting sun, I looked at Kua then at Mama and knew they, too, felt a sudden presence...then we heard the flapping of wings and an owl swooped low across the lanai flying in the direction of the horizon...Buzz's aumakua, or guardian! Grandma's stories of the old Hawaiians' spiritual beliefs in guardian angels came immediately to mind. When Buzz was born, an owl kept hovering over the house as though protecting the newly born baby.

Thankfully, your thoughtful wire started Mama on lengthy tales of your youthful antics, which even brought a smile. He was such a wonderful brother...how lucky could a girl have been! Living and practicing in Honolulu, it was hard for him to get away, but he did try to come up to Kauai whenever he could. He had such a comfortable home of his own, and how he loved his garden. Fortunately, he was able to lure one of the boys on the ranch to come and take care of the house and garden for him and get in some riding when they could. However, he sure could have done with a permanent female touch.

Sara and Buzz were so much in love and she was perfect for him. Her dad was one of the few missionary descendants who went into politics and ended up being appointed governor of the territory. Mr. Carrington and Papa were solid political allies. Sara's family had a ranch on Molokai and they divided their time between that island and Oahu, somewhat like our family, actually. She was a bit younger than Buzz and had been educated in the East so knew a few of his friends. You must have met her along the way, too.

The other day Fusako was dusting the piano keys and there was a sudden rippling sound...my heart absolutely stood still. I couldn't help it. I dissolved in tears. Do you remember how he'd sit at the piano and just rattle off songs from off the top of his head..."Just one of those things," "Stormy Weather," "Body and Soul," Fats Waller tunes? Oh, the agony and the ecstasy of the memory! Ever since I was a baby, I can remember him playing the guitar or piano and singing to me. I never see sheep but what I think of those poor Eli lads he sang of. Do you play the piano?

Fusako could feel my sadness and came to enfold me in her arms to console me. She first came to the ranch house when only a few months old, strapped to her mother's back with an old obi while she did the laundry. Then at 15 she started as an upstairs maid and later became nursemaid for Buzz and me. She enjoyed her household duties but much preferred pinning up her kimono sleeves and puttering in the "chop suey" garden she created. What a devoted soul she is to the family, mainly due to the fact she never married and never had children of her own. Buzz's death brought us even closer.

As you can imagine, Buzz had his affairs pretty much in order. There was a very recent letter from you amongst his things in the hospital and I did start to read it to see who it was from. I promise I didn't read very far! I must say, though, that your techniques of writing are endearing. What a good friend you were and now are. Your taking the time to write to me means so much, too, and hope we may continue to keep in touch. We would love it so if you and Lucy could come out to visit us.

I thought it better to leave my job in Honolulu to be with Mama. Actually, it wasn't any big thing, and there is so much I can do here now. Maybe sometime later I will look around, either in Honolulu or here. I still am a little numb, too, but I know he's with God, and very much around us.

Mama has her moments when her grief overtakes her, but her faith is very strong. Buzz was her firstborn, and I always sensed that he came first in her life, too...after Papa, of course...but I never felt any kind of resentment or jealousy. She was always so proud of him, and he of her. He was there for her when Papa died so suddenly, so now I feel Buzz and Papa would want me here.

Buzz spoke of you so often I feel you are a part of our family. Your mother's letter was so touching. She really thought of him as a son, too. I'm sure that the outpouring of all the love and prayers sustained him at the end. His smiles radiated love and a sort of inner peace. Selfishly, I mourn him more than anyone will know...except maybe you, dear Pete.

> Fondly,
> Prudence Farnham

New York
May 24, 1952

Dear Prudence,

Lucy and Len are in Jamestown for the summer... lucky ones to escape the heat of New York. Since time hangs heavy, I can afford the luxury of leisurely answering your March letter that is here before me and let myself wallow in memories, times past, and the years I spent with your family in the '30s.

That summer of 1934 after we graduated from Kent

School, I finally got to visit Buzz in the Islands. I fell in love with Hawaii. It was love at first sight. That was the summer FDR paid a presidential visit to the Islands with Frankie and Johnnie in tow, and we were included in some of the younger set parties. What an introduction to the Islands! We had known the boys slightly through school, so it was rather amusing to us to see the Honolulu belles and their mothers vying for dates and attention. The presidential party and the Secret Service took over the whole top floor of the Royal Hawaiian Hotel. The elevators were closely guarded and restricted. Even Frankie and Johnnie had a hard time sneaking in and out to go cruising with the legendary beach boys after the formal parties.

Those summers with Buzz at your family's ranch on Kauai were some of the happiest times of my life. Each day I awoke to eagerly face a whole new world. Let's see, you were just a gangling tomboy...8, 9, 10...who loved horses and rode up into the mountains with the cowboys to pick maile and mokihana for those aromatic lei. Actually, we never really saw much of you, but the cowboys did!

Your mention of Kua brought back happy memories of a handsome Hawaiian cowboy. Remember when the dentist wanted to pull the last molar in his head? He protested and argued that it was his "pipikaula" tooth - you know, his chewing tooth! He was a born cowboy. A fine, handsome Hawaiian who prided himself especially on the rearing of the family's polo ponies. I remember riding in back of him on our way up to your family's rustic mountain cabin that you couldn't get to except by horseback. We spent several days there. It was a place apart. We seemed to be out of touch with the rest of the world. Kua taught Buzz and me the art of pig hunting, weaving fern lei for our hats, and listening for the songs of the land shells abounding in the forest. After a long day in the saddle, we hiked down to the waterfall to bathe in the icy cold mountain stream. Later over a few beers and dinner around the kerosene lamp, Kua began telling us stories of Kauai and Niihau. Imagine the Robinson family buying Niihau for $10,000 from Kamehameha III. Amazing that they still own the island now populated by only Hawaiians.

Sitting here thousands of miles away, I can still picture the motherly Japanese maid who used to take care of you. She was patience personified. And the Portuguese woman, Nellie! She was devoted to Buzz, and how he loved to tease her. The stories he told about their trip from San Francisco aboard a ship with a circus traveling to Honolulu were too good to be true. Nellie gave him a wad of gum she'd been chewing and told him to give it to the monkey. Buzz confided that he had never known mortal fear until watching the monkey take the gum and become enraged. And then the lion escaped from his cage and was loose on deck. Buzz said Nellie locked him in their cabin and fingered her rosary until the lion was captured.

Do peacocks still roam through the gardens?

The Fourth of July holiday is coming up, and I'll be going up to join the family in Jamestown for the festivities, but nothing can ever compare to the 4th of July celebration in Honolulu when we were college lads. The world was our platter; we had the "world on a string" as the song goes. Those Fourth of July parties at your family's sprawling home on the water's edge at the foot of Diamond Head with the spectacular fireworks exploding out over the ocean were fabulous. However, the noise did set the dogs to barking, and I think it was your grandmother's pet Pekinese that yapped her way to exile! I can almost smell the ginger and pikake lei the girls wore as we danced the nights away under the stars at the Royal Hawaiian Hotel, famed for its romantic setting on Waikiki beach.

Yes, the summer days I spent at the ranch and then the

active social life in Honolulu interspersed with hard fought polo games at Kapiolani Park with visiting teams from Maui, the mainland, and Argentina went all too quickly. Is the Diamond Head house still there? We didn't know just how lucky we were to be in Hawaii during those pre-War days.

How well I remember throwing my lei overboard from the old Malolo as we sailed by your house to ensure my return. Buzz would laugh at me and then signal to you by flashing a mirror in response to your waving a sheet on the front lawn of the house. Your mother used to refer to those shipboard romances as "love between breakfast and lunch".

Your parents, your mother especially, were always so kind and hospitable to this Easterner turned native. There was a certain charm about her...maybe it was her Hawaiian blood...but her tranquil beauty and regal poise seemed to reflect a unique person. She always pooh-poohed us when we mentioned her royal ties, but she did have a commanding, yet gracious, air. I remember asking Buzz to give me a blood transfusion so I could say I was part Hawaiian.

Buzz and I often talked of my living in the Islands so we could go into business together, but then I became embroiled in the family's law business and now my excuse for settling in the Islands is gone. God rest his soul...I miss him.

Sincerely,
Pete

Kauai
July 14th, 1952

Dear Pete:

Your nostalgic letter of May is still here on my desk. How I wish I'd been six years older to have enjoyed your fantasy world in those days. I always hated it when Fusako led me upstairs to bed early just as you and Buzz were leaving for some exciting party.

Yes, the Diamond Head house is still there but has been sold and re-sold several times. Each time a bit of the land was sold off to neighbors, until now that beautifully designed Hawaiian style house with its unique roof line is almost cheek to jowl with adjoining modern houses.

Interesting that you mentioned Mama's being part-Hawaiian. Yes, she has all the best Hawaiian traits...beauty, grace, charm, poise, and how she loves life! In the years after WWI when Mama was growing up, there was a certain stigma to being part-Hawaiian that actually still remains somewhat today. Even though Mama was only a quarter Hawaiian on her mother's side, with an English father, she was always conscious of her place in society while growing up, even though some of her closest friends were haole...especially at Punahou School, founded by missionaries in Honolulu. The social life in Hawaii was dominated mainly by influential old missionary families whose children intermarried to produce more "cousins" to stand at their annual meetings. I guess no one ever told you that Kua was Mama's first cousin.

Sometimes I wonder how Papa ever came to settle in Hawaii since he came from a very proper New England Quaker family steeped in formal traditions. He came to Hawaii seeking his fortune in a new land and through hard work, honesty, and a pleasing personality soon built up a career in the investment field. He knew Hawaii was where he wanted to be and enjoyed both his work and the social life the Islands had to offer.

The Republican Party ruled throughout the Territory of Hawaii, and the "Big Five" ran the business world and the satellite sugar plantations situated mostly on the outer islands. Plantation managers were referred to as "kings" by the laborers. Living on isolated spots, these men ruled a small community and were given every perquisite to keep them happy, including a large house with ample servants (with their own cottages), tennis courts, pools, and guest cottages. This is where inter-island travelers who arrived by boat stayed until the ship returned in four or five days.

Well-established in business and the community, Papa fell hopelessly in love with Mama...two complete opposites but devoted to one another. Even though he adored my mother, her Hawaiian relatives were quite another thing. Once they were married, my father made it very clear that Mama have no contact with them or encourage our associating with them. Mama was torn, naturally, having come from a close family, and I am forever thankful that she showed her inner strength by defying Papa in this one instance only and we were able to know our wonderful grandmother. It was she who lived on Kauai and gave the ranch to my mother in trust for us children after Grandpa died and it became too much for her to manage.

I often wonder how Mama coped with her new position in Honolulu society after marrying Papa. My cousin, who was attending Notre Dame School in Belmont, CA when Mama and Papa visited in San Francisco, told me that Mama was always so kind to her and any other kids from Hawaii. She'd have them to their suite at the St. Francis Hotel, take them shopping after lunch or to a play, and they just loved being with her. Once back at the hotel with Papa and his friends, Mama seemed to become shy and unsure of herself. But that was long ago, thanks be!

Papa must have been very sensitive to the Hawaiian issue and quite aware of his fellow haole condescending attitude towards Hawaiians at the time of their romance because years later when I was about 17 or 18, he called me into his study and had a few words of advice I've never forgotten. "Don't forget you have Hawaiian blood in your veins," he began. "Not much, maybe, but enough to lead men into thinking they can take advantage of your lovable nature. Always be aware of this and remain the lady. You will never regret it." He laughed and added, "Let your missionary friends have 'one too many drinks,' but always watch your p's and q's so no one can raise an eyebrow in alluding to your Hawaiian blood."

Actually, Pete, I had and have a great role model in Mama!

Papa was on the strict side, but never really showed his disappointment when Buzz decided to become a doctor instead of becoming a partner in his prestigious investment company. After finishing medical school, and his internship, he went into obstetrics and gynecology and settled in Honolulu. Buzz and Papa always enjoyed a great friendship, probably beginning back in their polo playing days, and was with Papa at his untimely death that left us all devastated. He was there for Mama.

How did I get off on this track? Sorry! You're so easy to "talk to"!

We've spent a good part of July in Honolulu but have finally finished the painful chore of closing Buzz's house and dispensing with his personal possessions. It was only natural that he left the house to Kapiolani Hospital, an institution he was devoted to and where Grandma had served as a trustee for so many years with Queen Kapiolani, the founder. He requested that Sara and Mama take whatever they wanted from the house. With the exception of few sentimental family pieces of furniture, artifacts that belonged to Grandpa, valuable Hawaiian books and a painting by the favorite Island painter Howard Hitchcock, which belonged to Grandma, the rest was disposed of for the benefit of the Cancer Society.

Mama and I knew that you had a beautiful brown feather hat lei, but we want you, especially, to have Buzz's blue pheasant hat lei. Also we are sending you albums he kept of your prep school and college days...do what you will with these priceless relics! You'll have some real laughs! Hopefully, you will wear the studs and cufflinks Papa gave Buzz for a graduation present from prep school and remember all those proms and balls.

Naturally, Mama carries her grief with her and breaks down at odd times, but between her roses and activities at St. John's church she keeps fairly busy. We are in the midst of working with the designer for a small stained glass window for the church in Buzz's memory. I think Mama will feel close to him here, too.

As you can see I am still here on Kauai. Thank goodness for my horses! We can gallop across the pastures and spend our pent up energies and I can cry or laugh in the face of the wind. It is a glorious feeling. But now I miss my brother by my side. Mama tells me that when I was still a babe in arms Buzz used to sling me over his saddle and pay absolutely no attention to her pleadings and warnings. Later I remember holding on for dear life and loving every minute of his galloping rides. I rather hated getting my own horse.

Rumblings of Hawaii becoming a state are rumored around. Personally, I can't see us becoming a state with all the ramifications it involves. Since that takeover of the young Democrats after the end of WWII, there are some ambitious younger men of Oriental ancestry rising in the political world. Papa wouldn't have liked the business scene today with labor's grip on the Islands, the strikes, and the new breed of Democratic politicians. But, if at all, statehood is a long, long way off!

Hope your holiday in Jamestown was relaxing and fun.
Mama sends her love, too.

Fond Aloha,
Prudence

P.S. No, the peacocks became too noisy and tangled once too often with the dogs.

New York
September 2, 1952

Dear Prudence:

Where does the time go? Seems impossible your letter has been sitting here pending for three months. Mentally, I've written you many times, but that's no excuse, so please forgive the rude silence — and for not writing you also after receiving the blue pheasant lei, cuff links, and the albums. Of course, I wrote your mother immediately but put off writing you because I like to linger over these! The albums are priceless!!! I should have them insured! The cuff links are prized possessions, but I must tell you about the lei.

The other day I was in the elevator of the stock exchange and felt this fine looking elderly gentleman eyeing me and my hat. When we stepped out together, he turned to me and asked, "Pardon me, but are you from Hawaii?" I explained the circumstances and it turned out that he knew your father, a Mr. Shaw. Interesting.

I can't tell you the number of old pals who have called or written to inquire about Buzz after reading his obit in the alumni news bulletins. You'd be so proud to hear all the good things they've had to say about the guy. Repeatedly, it was..."Why so young?" Actually, I think we're thinking about our own selves. Some of the escapades recalled should help to make me, at least, a more tolerant father.

As a great tribute to an outstanding guy, our class at the university is instigating a medical school scholarship in his memory. I am only sorry that I didn't think of this myself, but am helping all I can with details now. It will be in his name, and your mother will soon be receiving all the information.

Personally, I probably would have thought of something more in the athletic line, which particular sport I wouldn't or couldn't really say, as he was so proficient in so many. But truthfully a medical scholarship is so much better and something he would have wanted. I only say sports because I have never forgotten how impressed we both were that evening we had cocoa with Father John (anything to get out of study hall). It was just the three of us around the fire in his study; he spoke informally of communication with and the manifestation of God. He said it came through sportsmanship. "The universe is a great playing field for life. The creator is showing us how the game of life can be played...the rules, the breaks, the goals, etc." There followed a far-reaching discussion.

Buzz always carried these thoughts with him, not only with his sportsmanship but also throughout his life. One of the guy's greatest virtues was that he realized that the friendships made at school needed working on to be continued...communication he called it, a two-way street. Remarkable how he kept in touch through letters, phone calls, and rare visits. But he did keep in touch, and this scholarship is a manifestation of that virtue.

As long as the weather holds, we try to get out to Lucy's family in Greenwich for relaxing weekends. I have a tough case going on now, and I must admit I get home late and tired which doesn't go over too well with Lucy, natch! Thankfully, we live in the city and can visit in Greenwich where so many of our contemporaries live. The guys don't mind the commute, but that would interfere with my seeing Len. I call her my sweet, blond beauty. The "terrible twos" hasn't really applied here – yet! I only hope and pray that she will eventually have a brother or two who will be as devoted and loving as yours.

How we'd love to come out to the Islands. Lucy has never been back since her stopover in 1936. Honolulu was their last port of call, so they stayed quite a while. If and when the opportunity arises, I shall grab it and give you plenty of time to weave the old hospitality mat, believe me. Washington is beckoning and the offer is tempting, but I have more or less made up my mind to remain in New York. A real Easterner, Lucy takes a dim view of moving in to that scene...maybe she's right.

My fondest regards to your dear mother, and you never answered my question...may I be your big brother?

With sincere regards,
Pete

Kauai
November 9th, 1952

Dear "Brother Pete":

There... does that answer your question! It sounds good, too. I like it.

Mama and I are deeply touched and thrilled over the scholarship. Exactly what he would have wanted, I know. She has received ever so many letters from his old school pals and teachers, too, and this has been a great solace to her. Some of the reminiscences are nostalgic and even funny. Why is it that one has to die before we realize how much they meant in our lives? Oh, if we would only just take the time to tell them or drop them that note we meant to.

Thought I'd share some of the letters with you. Ed Greer wrote: "Mr. Farnham and Dad had gone to Harvard together, and I shall always remember that most hospitable visit in your home at the foot of Diamond Head for cocktails with my family. It was the first time I'd seen a hikiee covered with layers of soft lauhala mats and piled with pillows. Buzz was quick to take me under his wing and was responsible for all the good times I had in Hawaii. When we sailed on the S.S. Lurline, my parents had a farewell cocktail party in their suite with their favorite Hawaiian music boys and those amusing beach boys. So many lei! I remember your mother coming early and bringing my mother a dozen strands of pungent pikake lei wrapped Hawaiian style in a ti-leaf puolo.

"As the ship turned in the harbor, we looked down and saw Buzz and his friends waving madly from a sleek speed boat crisscrossing the ship's path. We all threw our lei down to their outstretched arms as we steamed out of the harbor, and they followed us as far as the Royal Hawaiian until the ship picked up steam, blared its whistles and plowed ahead.

"To me, Buzz was Hawaii!"

Tim Wright wrote: "My mother remembers meeting you and Mr. Farnham at the opening of the Royal Hawaiian Hotel in 1928. She was struck by your beauty and grace and gracious hospitality in your lovely home. So several years later, she was delighted to have Buzz stay with us in Hillsborough on his way home from college. She always said he was such a charming young man with gentle Island ways and was always happy to have him as part of the family. The welcome mat was always out for Buzz whenever he came through San Francisco."

In his letter to Mama, Bunny Hopkins wrote: "Although I've never been to the Islands, I learned all about them through my friendship with Buzz at prep school and college. I first met him in Bermuda. He was with a group of kids from Hawaii who were spending their Easter vacation...very well chaperoned by Eastern relatives. I always admired their happy-go-lucky personalities and they were all so attractive, with an aura of innocence. They never seemed to get enough of the sun and ocean and spent days bicycling around the island and spending hours at the beach."

Mama is trying to answer each letter as they come in.

I try to keep busy but you can ride just so much, and the household seems to run smoothly, but I do yearn for some young companionship not to mention a play or symphony. I wouldn't even consider thinking of leaving now even though there seems to be a stream of visitors and considerate local friends who are good company for Mama. It's not the same.

The son of our retired ranch doctor has just returned from completing his residency and wants to be a family practitioner like his father here in the Islands. Since there are far fewer ranch people living on the property now, Dr. Paoa thought it was a good time to retire and felt the people would be happy with the doctors at the nearby west side Waimea Hospital. However, it's not the same. He knew each ranch family intimately and was on call day and night to go with his trusty little black bag. We were all so relieved when he chose to continue living here.

Anyway, Alika and I have had a few laughs, and I feel relaxed around him. Socially there isn't too much excitement on Kauai, but we have shared some super rides and beach picnics. Alika is about five years younger than Buzz...a great athlete, handsome and has the most beautiful brown eyes. He plays his guitar at every opportunity, and you can almost reach up and pick a star when listening to him. Mama thinks I enjoy his company more so because he was so devoted to Buzz. When they were younger, Alika used to tag along behind him, hanging on his every word. You'd be the first to know if it became serious, but I rather doubt it!

Alika graduated at the top of his class from Kamehameha School in Honolulu, founded by Princess Pauahi for her people, and won a scholarship to Stanford...pretty outstanding for an Island boy! Whenever Buzz was here, I remember him talking seriously to Alika so I'm not surprised he ended up in medical school.

On the other hand, there is that young intern down at the hospital who fancies himself quite a lady-killer from Milwaukee. It's just lucky for him my brother wasn't around the other night. My old school chums have written urging me to come East. How I would love nothing better and wish I could talk Mama into going. Even an old New York beau wrote and dangled dinner at "21" and any play I wanted to see. Maybe later.

Maybe all these memories have made me...well...not depressed, but thinking more of myself and my life selfishly. Somehow I feel that Papa would have politely frowned on my seeing so much of Alika.

Sorry to unburden myself but am so grateful for a ready ear, and if you're going to be my "brother," I can feel better about discussing my thoughts with you...thankfully. Sorry. I'll pick myself up.

John and Robert have asked us to have Thanksgiving dinner with them at Hale Kai. They have both been so thoughtful, and Mama and I look forward to being in that heavenly spot on the crescent bay and having a tour of the exquisite gardens they have created over the years.

Happy Thanksgiving...we have so much to be thankful for,

haven't we!! My fondest love to you and Lucy.
"Gobble, gobble, the turkeys are in trouble."

Much love,
Prudence

New York
December 3, 1952

Dear Prudence:

The snow is falling and I'm sitting here in front of the fire remembering the view from your lanai. I just want to get off a quick message to you, my dear girl, even though I know Lucy sent the family card...well, at least the picture of Len was good.

As I look back over this year, I see quite a few rough spots, but I agree, we have so much to be thankful for. I give thanks for men like your brother and that my life has been enriched from having known him. They say crying is unmanly...but you never know until sadness darkens your life...I know. I still can't believe he is gone. I feel as though I could call him and he'd always be right there to help me or to just have fun. I give thanks that God didn't let him suffer too long but allowed him to live a full life doing mostly for others. And isn't this what life is all about? We mustn't mourn, but rejoice in the true spirit of Christmas.

Brother Pete sounds good to me, too. I know how Buzz loved you and hope I can intuitively help you in any way, as he would have. This is my Christmas present to you, dear Prudence.

Alika sounds like a fine person, and I'm happy you have someone you enjoy. I can understand his friendship with Buzz, too.

This letter brings all my love and best wishes to you for a Merry Christmas. Please try, dear Prudence, to enjoy the holidays even though I know how hard it will be at times. I will be sending "these thought" waves all Christmas Eve and Day...so keep the channels open.

And here's to 1953! Let's make a toast to a year bright and happy with lots of good health.

Devotedly,
Pete

P.S. Hope Santa finds you!!!

Kauai
December 20th, 1952

Dear Pete:

Here it is almost Christmas. I can't let any more time slip by without stopping to write you a special letter full of good wishes, love, and cheer. The first Christmas without a loved one is always hard, but more and more we feel the true joys and wonders of this joyous season with each passing day...and we have people like you who have made it so with your sympathy and thoughtfulness.

The stained glass window is in and is truly magnificent, yet simple...the tree of life. The reds remind me of the colors in the cathedral in Chartres. Incidentally, did you ever walk the labyrinth there? Fascinating, but sometimes frustrating. The window will be dedicated in Buzz's memory the afternoon of Christmas Eve at the traditional children's service. I don't know whether I can keep back the tears...I've always shed tears of joy, anyway, but this year it will be doubly meaningful.

The simple five o'clock candlelight service is especially for the children, parents, grandparents, and anyone who cares to come and celebrate earlier than the midnight mass. The children bring presents wrapped in white and lay them in a manger. Believe me, they realize it is the Christ child's birthday and Santa has nothing to do with this joyful scene.

Mama has been potting some of her prize roses, and if you can believe it, the red beauties are in bud and should be perfect to bring into the little church that day. Would you say the hand of God?

She is more or less her old self, and for this I am most grateful. She is so appreciative of all the support from so many friends. We shall miss that "big hulk" dragging in the tree and setting it up "his way" and paying absolutely no attention to anyone else! He'd go as far as stringing the lights, that was it. Then he'd dash to the piano and play for hours while we merrily trimmed the tree. Such a fun time. Yesterday Fusako, Inoa, the old cowboy, and I quietly put up a tree and decorated it, but with these 12 foot ceilings it still had to be a tall tree. So many happy memories when we brought out each treasured ornament.

Through this quietness and peace I think the true meaning of the Christ child's birth is coming through loud and clear. This year the presents I have given are meaningful ones and not merely obligatory. Funny how from sheer habit we exchange presents and knock ourselves out to get the right thing for someone we seldom see anymore.

Sara will be here with us on Tuesday the 23rd through the first of the year. She and Buzz used to ride up in the mountains to pick maile for lei to drape over the grandfather clock and Grandpa and Grandma's portraits, so we're delighted that she still wants to share Christmas with us. We'll have the usual Christmas Eve dinner here, and I'm

afraid Matsu always goes overboard in the food depart-
ment but loves the exciting challenges. She's long since
made the plum puddings and wrapped them in brandy. Oh,
yes, she will make your favorite taro cakes. She remembers
your devouring them and was always so proud of that! New
Year's is the traditional time for the Japanese to celebrate, so thankfully the help will be here over Christmas
and off over the New Year.

Since Alika will be home, Mama has suggested asking
him to the services and dinner later. So with the young
doctor, who interned with Buzz and has come to work in
the emergency room at the hospital, and Mama's longtime
girlhood friend, Anna, and her husband, we'll be seven...eight
if the minister can come.

Alika's parents Kawika and Lei Paoa have kindly invited
Sara, Mama, and me to their New Year's Eve paina. Super
Hawaiian food at the gathering of the old timers and their
families. Mama is rather looking forward to such a happy
occasion with old friends she remembers from childhood. Of
course, I'm very pleased.

In the meantime, Mama and I will have the ranch hands
and their families in for the traditional distribution of presents and bountiful refreshments. It's a festive custom
Grandpa started years and years ago, and now Mama
wants it continued. Kua plays Santa and the children go
wild with excitement.

With Christmas and New Year's falling on a Thursday,
this makes for two long holiday weekends for everyone on
the ranch. The Hawaiians have always tended to make more
of a celebration of New Year's rather than Christmas, so
this year they can really relax and enjoy. I can remember
Grandma telling us that as children they looked forward
more to celebrating the New Year. The house was cleaned,
everyone had new homemade outfits, including hats made

of local fiber, and people went from house to house to call on New Year's Eve. Everyone cooked for days, preparing for the feasting at midnight that continued until dawn. People loved going from house to house exchanging greetings, singing, and dancing. Christmas didn't officially come to Honolulu until 1862 so it took some time for the rituals and customs of the season to reach the outside Islands.

The weather is nippy for Christmas, and a roaring fire at night is welcome. Heaven knows there's enough wood on the property to keep us going.

And so Merry, merry Christmas...merry, merry everything to you, Lucy, and Len. God bless you all and may the New Year hold all sorts of good things for all of us!!!

As always,
Prudence

CHAPTER II

New York
January 1, 1953

Prudence, dear:

Happy New Year!!!

Oh, so happy to have your Christmas card with the view down to the ocean from the lanai. What memories.

We had a busy but joyous Christmas here at home...lots of excitement, wrapping paper, and toys, but then Christmas is for children! Len loves the blanket your mother so kindly knitted for her and goes to sleep cuddling up with as many dolls and animals as she can gather up under the warmth of that blanket! I tell her it's from her "Tutu" in Hawaii, whom she will meet someday and that Aunt Prudence will take her swimming on beautiful beaches.

Celebrated New Year's in Chestnut Hill with my family who send their best regards. There are still quite a few of my old cronies living around Philadelphia so with doting grandparents available for baby sitting we had some jolly reunions.

Busy times now catching up at the office, but our big news at home is that Lucy is...what did we say...hopi? Anyway, barely three months, but we're both ecstatic. Poor Len hasn't felt the pinch yet.

In haste, but wanted you to know you are in my thoughts as always.

Devotedly,
Pete

P.S. How I thought of you New Year's Eve enjoying all that succulent Hawaiian food, especially the pig cooked underground in the imu! Who got the tail? Wasn't it meant to bring good luck in the coming New Year? Some day I'll be there to reach for it, too!

Kauai
January 16th, 1953

Dear Pete:

Happy New Year!

So exciting about Lucy being "hapai"! Will have to take some knitting lessons from Mama! Incidentally, I framed the family Christmas card and have it right here on my desk so I can look into your beaming faces as I write you.

We had a lovely holiday, and I loved your dear letter. The service Christmas Eve seemed more beautiful than ever before, and as we knelt and sang, "Silent Night," I looked up at the window and thought of Buzz. He used to nudge me to remind me that he had taught me how to play this on the piano with one finger when I could barely reach the keyboard. I couldn't keep back the tears.

On a happier note, a very exciting and happy turn of

events is transpiring! A few days before Christmas Sara and I joined Alika to ride up into the mountains to pick maile to make lei for Buzz's grave. Later it was rather touching when the three of us placed the lei on the tombstone of someone we each had loved in our own special way. A few nights later Alika picked Mama, Sara, and me up to go to the ranch manager's open house, and in deference to our guest, Mama and I sat in the back seat.

When next the three of us met for a picnic at the mountain house, I felt like the third party, and New Year's Eve, when I watched Alika playing and singing to Sara, I knew a spark had been kindled! Yes, by the time they left for Honolulu together on Monday, there was no mistaking that smoldering spark. I feel no remorse or unhappiness, only joy for Sara and Alika. I'm grateful there was never a serious moment or commitment between Alika and me. I think he filled a void in my life when I needed it the most, and this budding romance makes all of us happy. Since they are both in Honolulu, at least until Alika decides on his practice, they will be able to see one another and get to know each other. I will keep you posted on the progress!

The Paoa's New Year's Eve party was a festive climax to a sad year. Mama surprised us all by staying up to sing "Auld Lang Syne"...I'm sure the tears came later, but this is a great step and think she felt so at home and relaxed with her old aikane...friends, in case you've forgotten your Hawaiian. Since Papa's death, I notice that she prefers Kauai and renewing friendships here, rather than visits to Honolulu, which have become fewer and fewer.

Incidentally, the food was the best ever, right from the imu to the table and kept us busy for quite a while! Oh, how we loved hearing all the old Hawaiian songs the boys played, some naughty, some sad, but always melodious. There were even a few hula, too. So everyone welcomed in 1953 with joy.

The other night I broached the subject of going to Hono-lulu and taking some art courses, and even though Mama thought it a good idea, she really didn't have her whole heart and soul in that one. Maybe I should slowly start in-stigating the idea of a trip East or even Europe. Physically she's more than up to either, and the change would do her so much good...maybe I'll try it later.

Winter may be here but the huapala (sweetheart) vine is in full bloom and spreading its vivid orange blossoms over fences and up to the top branches of the tallest trees! Quite a sight! And the cup-of-gold bushes in between the royal palms are in full bloom all up the driveway to the house. I'm sure even nature is heralding a great new year!

This brings ever so much love to all of you. Take care of Lucy!!!

> Fondly,
> Prudence

New York
February 4, 1953

Dear Prudence:

Yes! By all means start planting the seeds of travel...even just a trip to New York for a change of scenery, and, of course, for us all to be together. Please don't put it off too long as Lucy's due date is in late June or early July and things will be a bit uncertain after that. But just the thought of seeing you and your mother has prompted this speedy reply.

And as for the romance, I suppose it was only natural that Alika and Sara should meet, and through their mutual love of Buzz feel a special closeness. They seem to have a lot in common, too, both being raised on outside island ranches.

Who knows, Alika might decide to practice on Molokai if things become serious. I wonder how much that island has changed; hopefully, the medical strides in the treatment of leprosy have erased the stigma of the disease attached to that island.

It was in the mid '30s when Buzz and I went to Molokai, and I especially loved the east end of the island, although we were guests of Jim Coke on the west end of the island. It was great deer country, and I learned to throw a net to catch fish in the lagoon in front of the family's beach cottage. We were at a big rodeo in Kaunakakai when Warner Baxter, a movie star of the day, appeared with his host. Later a fellow guest, Andy Anderson, wrote the song, "The Cockeyed Mayor of Kaunakakai" in his honor.

Come to think of it, it must have been Sara's family's ranch lands we rode through to get to the heavenly Halawa Valley on the east end. Is the hula bridge still swaying over the chasm? I remember the ranch lands rolled from the hills down to the rocky cliffs and crashing waves. The ranch even had its own airstrip. The kukui grove on the property was considered the second most sacred heiau in the islands. According to the old Hawaiians, if you walked in and broke a branch or even a twig, you were inviting the wrath of the Hawaiian gods. Buzz confirmed the superstition by telling about a guest who defied the laws by walking boldly through the grove of trees. That evening she suffered back pains and had to be flown to the doctor in Honolulu. We never loitered long outside, either, as it had an eerie sense of foreboding stillness. Funny I should remember this even today.

Please know that I shall be thinking of you and your mother on the 12th with great compassion and love. The first anniversary is a difficult milestone.

The scholarship fund is receiving pledges all the time, even some of the boys from prep school want to contribute.

The Zetes of our class have all been heard from. Isn't that remarkable! Jim Tompkins is a great investment man and is handling that part of it, so we should be very solid financially, too.

Unfortunately, I have to go down to Washington next week on a very confidential mission which may last a couple of weeks. Lucy isn't very happy about it, as you can imagine, but what can you do when the President himself calls the troops? Lucy's old Nanny, Miss Crowe, is coming to stay in the apartment which relieves my mind somewhat. My mail will be forwarded just in case you feel like writing. Washington can be a lonely place.

No, I didn't think your heart was really in the relationship with Alika, and I'm delighted that you're happy with the turn of events. You deserve only the best!

> Fondly,
> Pete

Kauai
February 18th, 1953

Dear Pete:

How dear of you to send Mama that beautiful spring bouquet which arrived the morning of the 12th after we returned from church and putting lei on Buzz's grave. Mama was so touched, it brought tears to her eyes. She placed it beside his picture on her dressing table...the one in his polo duds leaning against the wind on the mallet.

She thought she was alone in her grief, but a week or so before the 12th, Mama's dear friend, Anna, remembered, too. She asked us to come to dinner quite casually with some old friends of Dan's from the East who turned out to be charming. Can you believe...parents of Dan Fuller who was in prep school with you and Buzz! Small world. So we've weathered another hurdle.

So much has been going on since then, please forgive me for not writing sooner. The family's good friend, Sam King, was appointed our territorial governor by President Eisenhower, and we're all pretty proud of the fact that he is the Island's first part-Hawaiian governor. He kindly sent us special invitations to his inauguration ceremony and the ensuing festivities. Since Mama hadn't been to Honolulu for over a year, except on brief business trips, she was a bit hesitant about going, especially with the crowds and seeing old friends, but we went!

The day was made for the swearing-in ceremony on the grounds of Iolani Palace and I was so proud of Mama, so happy to see all her old Honolulu friends at the reception that followed at Washington Place. The next evening we had a quiet dinner with the King family, and Mama was thrilled to be there in Queen Liliuokalani's former home... now the governor's mansion.

We stayed several days at the Halekulani Hotel, and everyone was so eager to please and concerned for Mama's welfare that it seemed like our home away from home. Their famous popovers are still as high and fulfilling as ever, and the parade along the sea wall of people of various shapes in all manner of dress or near un-dress is never ending amusement. We had Sara and Alika for dinner at the hotel one night, and I can honestly report to you that the romance seems pretty serious and obvious, especially while sitting outside of the House Without A Key (made famous by Charlie Chan) under the Kiawe tree for cocktails before dinner. The surfers and canoers were out in force to catch the last of the setting sun. Those attractive women in holoku with flowers in their hair seemed to play and sing just for us.

It did Mama good to see old friends, and we even took in a Community Theatre play. But she was ready to get home to her weekly meeting of older women on the ranch who are working on a Hawaiian quilt while discussing different aspects of Hawaiiana...art, culture, medicinal plants, lomilomi (massage), beliefs, the art of Huna, and it's fascinating to hear her report on their Hawaiian superstitions and their origins. One old-timer in the group interprets dreams, and it's amazing how close to the truth she has come. Maybe I'll sit in on some sessions...even though I barely can thread a needle.

Since Mama has had a change of scenery, maybe now is a good time to talk of traveling again. I'll be in touch if I have any luck! Honolulu was a great step.

Hope Washington's not too lonely!

Fondly,
Prudence

Washington D.C.
March 3, 1953

Dear Prudence:

A tourist I am not! But wanted to send this postcard from D.C. "with the proverbial greetings." We're knee deep in work, so no time to "gawk." Hope the seeds are sprouting.

Fondly,
Pete

Kauai
March 18th, 1953

Dear Pete:

Three nights ago over cocktails Mama dropped a bombshell. "What would you think of going East?" I didn't even have to plant a seed! She had received a letter from an old friend, recently widowed, who lives in Hobe Sound, Florida, asking her to come and visit. Obviously she had been thinking of this for several days as she continued. "I thought we could take a boat to San Francisco, stay at the St. Francis, do some shopping, and visit with Papa's cousins in Hillsborough before going to Florida.

"Then we could fly to New York for a few days before heading back West to take the ship back home."

It was hard to contain my excitement, but I managed somehow, and we discussed plans over dinner. So now she'll write Athalie Loomis and accept her invitation with dates, etc., alert the California relatives and I'll make arrangements!

When all is done, I'll send along our schedule so you can mark the New York dates in red!! We'll stay at the Plaza.

A warm and loving letter from Sara saying she was busy with her work at Honolulu Academy of Arts and loving it. Alika has accepted an offer to practice in a prestigious Honolulu medical group, so I suspect their relationship had a lot to do with his decision.

The 26th of April is Prince Kuhio's birthday and a holiday in the Islands. It's especially celebrated here on Kauai, his birthplace. The cowboys have organized a rodeo and roping events here at the ranch arena and Mama and I are ordering trophies. Their plans for a big barbecue as a finale sounds exciting, so I have something to look forward to beside my volunteer work at the Historical Society.

Loved your card...hope you've had some time to relax and hopefully you'll be headed home soon. I must write Lucy, too, when I know our dates, so we can have a "girlie lunch."

Fondly,
Prudence

Washington D.C.
March 31, 1953

Dear Prudence:

Your letter brought such good news, I danced down Constitution Avenue!!! Actually for two reasons...our work over here is, how do you say, "pau"? and I'm headed home tomorrow. Lucy was so happy to receive your letter and is looking forward to meeting you and having a quiet lunch. I gather she's quite outgrown the Chanel suits and says she'd like to at least look somewhat chic when she first meets you. You'll love one another.

It's been concentrated work with only a few days off to check on things in New York, and happy to report Miss Crowe has the situation well in hand.

Now we await your itinerary with great expectations!!! Hopefully your old beaus won't monopolize your time.

Lucy and Miss Crowe have been busy turning a guest room into the nursery, and she tells me, "with accents of blue". That would be nice, too, but just a healthy normal baby is what we both want.

So, dear Prudence, must get to my packing and so shall send lots of love, and here's to a great visit in our fair city!

Devotedly,
Pete

P.S. With all the excitement of your arrival, I forgot another very important thing I would like to do. The enclosed check hopefully covers an annual trophy in Kua's name. It would make me so happy to be a part of such an exciting event, as he contributed so much to my love of Hawaii and Kauai in particular.
Who knows, maybe some day I can give the award personally! Many thanks, dear Prudence.

As always with so many memories,
Pete

Kauai
April 19th, 1953

Dear Pete:

We're making real strides in plans, and I must say that when Mama makes up her mind... the action begins non-stop. So now I can send along a rough itinerary and dates for New York. I'm so excited! Mama begins to have misgivings at times, but I can always take care of that.

We sail from Honolulu May 16th on the S.S. Monterey and arrive San Francisco the 21st -where we'll be at the St. Francis Hotel until we leave for Hobe Sound May 31st. Mama thinks four days there is one too many... something about fish...but we'll leave for New York - flying to La Guardia on the afternoon of June fifth. Please don't even think of meeting us! It's peak traffic time and we have a limo reserved to take us to the Plaza. I'll call as soon as we get to our rooms.

To continue with the itinerary...we'll depart New York the evening of June 12th, spend the night of the 13th at the St. Francis and sail for Honolulu on the S.S. Lurline on the

14th. We'll fly back to Kauai the same day!!

New York! Can you stand it? I wrote Lucy and asked you both for cocktails the 7th with some old friends, and Lucy for lunch the 6th quietly with me. As I said to her, if she doesn't feel up to luncheon out, we could have it sent up to the suite. In any case, we have firm dates, and sometime I want to get to know little Miss Len, too.

Mama and I were so touched by your donating a trophy, and when we told the cowboys, they decided to surprise Kua at the rodeo and billed the award for the "under 20" roping event as the mystery award. How I wish you could have been here to give it yourself and share in all the excitement. However, I kept my eyes glued on Kua as the MC approached the microphone to announce the mystery award and winner of the event. Well, he sat there rather stunned when he announced, "The Kuakini Purdy perpetual trophy is warded to Johnny Appoliana"...Kua's favorite nephew!

Then his eyes popped, he stood up, waved his hat around, almost losing the fern lei in his enthusiasm, and started down the bleachers. I thought he was going to pop his buttons and hope the enclosed photos give you some idea of all the joy you added to such and exciting day. When we told Kua who had given it in his name, his eyes filled with tears, and of course, lots of stories of you and Buzz ensued.

So heartwarming! Consider yourself blessed.

If Madeline is still in residence at the Plaza, maybe Miss Len would like to come to tea! In any case, I want very much to spend some time with her!

Please put the dates down in red ink!!!

As always,
Prudence

New York
April 27, 1953

Dearest Prudence:

Lucy and I have the dates down in red ink on her calendar, mine, and the one in the kitchen, plus a big memo under many magnets on the refridge!!! We'll be waiting for your call.

Unfortunately, I couldn't get to the mayor to have him proclaim June 5th Farnham Day, but I did order the red carpet.

You're so considerate, and Lucy appreciates your having lunch at the hotel rather than at her club or some fancy restaurant. She isn't all that comfortable at this point even, but the doctor says she is doing very well.

Actually, I confess to you that the doctor didn't want her to have another baby this soon, but she wants several children, which is fine by me, and so he is keeping a special eye on her condition.

Many thanks for taking care of the trophy and reporting such a glowing account of the event. Kua is truly a Hawaiian treasure, and some day I wish he would sit still long enough to have an artist do either a sketch or portrait of him for me. As I've said before, Prudence, he was such a part of my life on Kauai. I enclose a copy of the touching letter he wrote me.

Park Avenue is a sea of color with all the spring flowers in bloom. Last week it was all tulips. We certainly don't want to monopolize your time but would love to have you here for dinner some night, too. Of course, your plans come first.

Things haven't slackened at the office, but I do try to get home at a reasonable hour to be with Lucy and Len as much as I can and weekends are reserved for Greenwich with her family.

Dear Prudence...it will be wonderful to see you after all these years. Oh, so many wonderful times to recall! I don't think I'll ever get Hawaii out of my blood. Those years in the Islands with Buzz really had a great influence on my life. I often wonder what would have happened if things had turned out differently and we'd gone into business together. But then my life now is one of supreme happiness, and I can keep the ties to Hawaii alive and warm by our correspondence. I hope you know that.

Please save yourself for New York. We have lots to catch up on. Bon voyage and don't talk to any strangers in airports!

Fondly,
Pete

Hobe Sound
May 4th, 1953

Dear Lucy and Pete:

Your exquisite roses were a heavenly welcome to San Francisco, and the scent was aromatic! Thoughtful as ever!

Here I am at our second stop languishing by the pool while Mama and Mrs. Loomis are at luncheon at the club. This is a lovely part of the world...watery, rather exclusive and intimate, but such hospitable people many of whom have been to Hawaii at one time or another. One of the daughters of our old Diamond Head neighbors has married and winters here.

The pseudo luau our hostess had to welcome us here was almost authentic, and she and her cook must have had several trial dinners to produce such a delectable meal and enjoyable evening.

Mrs. Loomis is such a dear person, and she and Mama seem to have so much to catch up on, chatting away like two old school girls. During the years her father, Admiral

Henkley, was stationed at Pearl Harbor, she attended Punahou School with Mama and they've kept in touch ever since with only occasional visits. So you can imagine the questions and answers. However, I do think Mama has convinced her to come out and spend some time on the ranch with us this fall or whenever she can. She's quite an equestrian, and I can just see her with Kua.

There is a most attractive young man here who has recently lost his wife, and you can imagine the number of casseroles being delivered by attractive unattached women. He was my dinner partner the other night and couldn't have been more attentive, although I know his heart wasn't really in it. But, goodness, he was so attractive! Are there any like this in New York who don't need casseroles!!!

San Francisco was glamorous as ever! The hallowed salons at Magnin's, cable cars clanging their way up and down those hills, the flower peddlers on the corners with those special gardenia corsages, Fishermen's Wharf with all those restaurants offering fresh seafood and the view of the busy harbor. Golden Gate Park was in full flower...oh, so enchanting! We enjoyed our shopping sprees and thanks to Mama's favorite saleslady of many years standing at Magnin's we were shown every courtesy and consideration so that our rooms were a sea of tissue paper for days!

The Hillsborough relatives came into the city and spent a whole day and evening with us so we could relax and catch up with family news. Then they gave us a lovely luncheon at the charming old Burlingame Club, the former home of William Crocker. Mama was so pleased to see several old friends including Tim Wright's parents, who are such an attractive couple.

The St. Francis is changing with the times and the institution of Monday luncheons at the "Frantic," when the ladies loved to be seen dining there to prove they weren't home doing laundry, are a thing of the past!

Now we look forward with great anticipation to our visit in New York and catching up with you and the little one. Mama joins me in sending our fondest aloha.

As always,
Prudence

P.S. Lucy, I hesitate to even ask you another favor, but because time is of the essence, could you possibly consider bringing Missy to the hotel about 10:30 or 11 on the 12th, our last day. Mama is anxious to get to know her and we could have a little tea party upstairs. Maybe you could ask her to bring some of her favorite animals or dolls to come to the tea party. We have a luncheon date at 1:00 with the Brakelys so will have lots of time for "our party" and will be ready to leave the hotel when the limo arrives to take us to the airport at 6. Of course, I'll understand if this is too much to ask.

One day we plan to spend the morning at the Frick Museum, which we both love. Mr. Frick's granddaughter was at boarding school the same time I was and I always envied her living in a museum...and what a museum! Mama seems to be loving the exciting times!

Love,
Prudence

New York
June 14, 1953

Prudence Farnham
S.S. Lurline
San Francisco, California

Lucy and the twins send their eternal love and gratitude
STOP All resting well at hospital STOP Probably for ten
days STOP Miss Crowe at apartment STOP Len hasn't
quite grasped the situation as yet STOP What would we
have done without your quick thinking and actions the 12th
STOP Happy to report Father holding up remarkably well
STOP Wish you were here to share some champagne STOP
Bon Voyage STOP

Fond Aloha,
Pete and Lucy

At sea en route to Honolulu
On board the S.S. Lurline
June 15th, 1953

Dear Lucy and Pete:

   Your welcome wire relieved our minds no end!!! Thankfully, we
made great connections with time to spare, but kept wondering
how things were progressing with you at the hospital.

   How fortuitous that we had our little tea party in our
rooms and Mama was able to stay with Len while we made
our hasty exit, Lucy! You were so brave and concerned over
Len's not being frightened. One minute we were laughing
over our teacups and the next minute I saw you clutching
your side with the most perplexed look on your face. I knew
something was wrong. Thanks be Mama had the presence

of mind to take Len into the other room, while I put you on the sofa and called that nice Doctor Harriman. He is such a gentleman, and his concern for your welfare ever evident as he told me exactly what to do and where to go.

Sorry I couldn't get a hold of you, Pete, but hopefully Miss Crowe succeeded in reaching you and you got to the hospital in time to be with Lucy reasonably soon. For once I was thankful for the cab driver's darting in and out of traffic. We even got there before the doctor. By three o'clock you were in hard labor, Lucy, and I was really worried. I didn't want to leave you and kept hoping you'd arrive, Pete, but I couldn't take any chances and knew you were in good hands with Dr. Harriman in attendance. I was so torn but couldn't take the chance of delaying the flight West.

Mama loved being with Len and they got along famously. I know she loved Len calling her "Tutu" and the role of grandma quite becomes her. The Brakelys were so considerate and came up to the room for lunch with Mama and were enchanted with Len. I don't think she was all that happy to see Miss Crowe arrive.

Twins!!! How exciting. Poor Pete. In your excitement you forgot to say...boys, girls, or one of each? I do hope labor didn't go on too long, and then to have not one, but two!

If only we'd had another day in New York, or we had had the tea party one day earlier. But thanks be all is well now and please send pictures of the happy family as soon as you're settled at home.

Oh, Lucy, it was wonderful getting to know you and hearing about the time you met Buzz in Honolulu and the fun times you had. Being with you both was the highlight of the trip for me.

There is quite a group of college kids returning home for the summer, and the ship resembles one big house party. The other night one of the lads (missionary stock) returning from Yale was having drinks out on deck and decided to toss his empty glasses overboard. Everyone thought it hilarious, but when he picked up a deck chair and heaved it overboard it wasn't quite that funny. Wouldn't want to be there when his father gets the bill. However, on the whole, they're quite a well-behaved, albeit romantic, group of handsome young people.

Don't suppose you and Buzz partook of any such escapades on your trips back and forth to Hawaii, Pete! Seems only yesterday that I was one of that group, too. I wonder what ever happened to that good-looking houseguest of one of the Cokes. His father was big in the steel business in PA and he was captain of the rowing crew at Yale.

Oh, the enormity of the twins just struck me full on!!! I'm sure the grandmothers had a great time doubling up on all the needed accessories that go with a 'surprise package.' Incidentally, Mama is knitting overtime now to finish one blanket and start on another.

Amazing how Matson Navigation Company always manages to have the most attractive young pursers. This one is rather attentive and dances divinely. So it makes it most enjoyable being seated at the Captain's table. The Captain remembers Mama and Papa from previous trips before WWII so is most attentive...and she rather enjoys it.

Just heard we are transferring an ailing passenger to the S.S. Mariposa, headed for San Francisco, so shall get this in the mailbag pronto.

Lots and lots of love to you both and hugs for the twins and Len!!

Fondly,
Prudence

New York
June 15, 1953

Miss Prudence Farnham
S.S. Lurline
En route Honolulu

Ooops STOP Think I forgot to add the twins identity STOP
Sorry STOP Girl and boy in that order STOP 18 hours of
labor but am recovering STOP Lucy ecstatic STOP
Harriman advises ten more days then home STOP Hope
you're having good weather and fun STOP

Fondly,
Pete

Kauai
July 7th, 1953

Dear Lucy and Pete:

Home safe and sound after our whirlwind trip, and New
York seems a million miles away! However, you are con-
stantly in my thoughts and never stop wondering how you
are coping with all the unexpected changes! You were so
thoughtful to send the second wire! How I wish I could see
Len with her brother and sister! One of each! I do hope you
were able to engage the nanny you were in touch with, especially after your eighteen hours of labor, Lucy. I'm quite certain letters will be few and far between with all you have to
do, but no news is good news. Now I definitely need an up-
date on the family photo here on my desk.

   Coming home by ship is always a thrilling experience, and
about the fourth day out of San Francisco it was fascinating to see the ocean change from deep blue to the soft Ha-

waiian greens, just as the officers change from the somber blue to the becoming white uniforms. And the flying fish! The day we arrived I was up even before the stars had faded just to be on deck in time to catch the first sign of Makapuu Point, Koko Head, and Diamond Head, the Sphinx-like guardian of the great Pacific. As we cruised along the shoreline, I could barely make out our old house now that there are so many other structures around it, but the pink Royal Hawaiian Hotel, dominated Waikiki Beach like the grande dame she is.

Then the ship slowed down as two tugs pulled alongside the open hatch to unload eager greeters laden with lei who couldn't wait for the ship to dock to welcome their friends, family, and the several notables and movie stars aboard. Dear Sara braved the Jacob's ladder with the assistance of two burly Hawaiian stevedores to welcome us home, and oh, how delicious those ginger lei smelled! As the ship eased along the pier, I couldn't help crying for joy when the Royal Hawaiian Band struck up "Aloha Oe" and Lena Machado's famous voice rang out! We were home!!!

We spent the night at the Halekulani Hotel so Mama could tend to some business at the Trust Company. Alika, handsome as ever, and Sara, happiness personified, came to dinner and we were able to catch up on each other's news. Alika remembers Dr. Harriman as an eminent OB man from his school days. They seem so relaxed and happy and hope to get to Kauai sometime soon which would be nice.

We received a warm welcome home from the faithful doxies who wouldn't leave our sides the rest of the day. The pungent stalks of yellow ginger abounding around the lanai are in full bloom. Can you remember the delicious fragrance that fills the air? That evening the cowboys gathered round the lanai to welcome us home with beautiful lei and their ukuleles and guitars to make heavenly music. There's nothing like a warm Hawaiian aloha from such lovable people. After our travels, it's rather nice to be back in a place where everyone knows one another and familiar faces are the norm!

Since our return, Hal Faye, the doctor who went to med school with Buzz has called several times when he has ample time off and we have enjoyed a few challenging rides. He's quite the equestrian and is fascinated with Kua's horsemanship and tales. I think he loves the relaxation and really appreciates the beauty that abounds, too. We went to a rousing 4th of July party over at Hanalei and met several of his fellow doctors who have moved here. However, Hal isn't sure whether he wants to settle on Kauai in his present capacity. E.R. duty isn't the easiest, but he likes the experience with its challenges and loves the island.

Sitting here looking out the window, I'm fascinated watching the winds drive the misty rain down the valley. It reminds me of some delicate scene on an Oriental screen. It's almost ethereal.

This brings so much love to all of you and hope things are settling down a bit by now.

Please give Len a big hug for me and pat the twins. Mama sends her love, too...still knitting madly.

As always,
Prudence

New York
September 8, 1953

Dear Prudence:

Where does the time go? Has it really been three months since you were here in New York, not to mention your last letter? The silence doesn't mean that we don't think of you often and love you, but as you say, the tempo at chez Thorne isn't the same, and we all sing to a new drummer...make that two! But it's wonderful to come home in the evening to my growing family and exuberant wife, who, incidentally, is spending most of her spare time at her desk. Lucy's room at the hospital resembled a combination flower-baby shop, and she's paying the piper now. Thank goodness we were able to engage the nanny who is a perfect jewel, and between her and Len, the twins are well cared for and on a happy schedule for all.

How brief but how sweet was your visit. It took me a while to adjust to the "grownup Prudence" and heartily approve. Lucy and I will be forever grateful to your cool presence of mind and loyalty to Lucy in her critical hour of need.

As Dr. Harriman explained it to me, the x-rays didn't show two, as Ian was snuggled firmly in back of Em, a shadow, which also caused some of the complications at delivery.

You can imagine my joy as I stood at the nursery window admiring my little girl and then the utter surprise when a nurse came scurrying down the hall to announce I was the proud father of a son also!! I was stunned and couldn't wait to see Lucy and rejoice twofold with her!

She hasn't been out much at all since that enjoyable cocktail party you and your mother had where we were delighted to discover we had so many mutual friends. Your dear mother is still the gracious hostess and has lost none of her grace and aristocratic charm.

Actually Lucy is practically back to normal, but Dr. Harriman wants her to take it easy. She can't wait to get back to her tennis...heat and all. New York in the summer isn't the most ideal place to be, and getting out to Greenwich is just a little too hectic at this point.

It was a great treat for us to have you and your mother quietly for dinner, and having seen the apartment, you can appreciate why we're looking for a larger place ! which we hope to find soon.

The papers are full of the Jackie/Jack wedding. Now there's a lad who knows where he's going.

We all send our fondest love, dear Prudence. In haste, but with enduring affection.

Fondly,
Pete

Kauai
November 1st, 1953

Dear Pete and Lucy:

The pictures arrived, and thrilled to have them...makes me want to fly off to New York to see for myself and give each of you a big hug. Have the best one of you all...Len trying to hold the twins...in the frame here on my desk.

Wanted to send special greetings for a blessed Thanksgiving...even though we have so much to be thankful for each day. We'll be going to Hale Kai again for Thanksgiving dinner and a tour of the gardens.

Have met an attractive young man, Larry Freeman from Boston, who has come to Kauai to be the golf pro at the local club. Having been raised in the city drenched in American lore, he's an avid history buff, and it's been fun sharing his enthusiasm for history of the island. He's good company but nothing romantic. Actually, I'm quite content with my life here even though friends in Honolulu and the mainland can't seem to understand how or why I remain on this small island with its lack of excitement and the stimulation of the art and theater a big city has to offer. Besides taking on more responsibility on the ranch, I'm able to read a lot. Have you read "From Here to Eternity" yet?

I like to keep in touch with so many of my friends through letters, and it's a great source of sharing the news in our lives. Sometimes, too, you can honestly say more in a letter than face to face by openly expressing your feelings. Through letters we recall and share happy memories that can be preserved for prosperity. I only hope my letters aren't too long and rambling, but since I treasure our friendship, it gives me real pleasure to be keeping in touch.

Just to assure you that I haven't become an introvert, I hasten to let you know that I volunteer at the hospital twice a week and my compassion for some of the patients leads to following through beyond hospital duties.

The sun has come out ! time to check the fences with Kua. He's such a rich treasure trove of "the good old days," and I really should write down some of his more memorable tales of the ranch. Sometimes when he's going on and on, I'm convinced the stories come from a vivid imagination, but Mama assures me they're true.

May God's blessings shine forth in your lives, and here's to a blessed Thanksgiving with family and friends.

Fondly,
Prudence

New York
November 19, 1953

Dear Prudence:

Lucy and Nanny are organizing the gigantic task of moving the troops to Greenwich for the week of Thanksgiving. Can you appreciate the action? So before I leave to join them in a few days, I wanted to get this letter off to you to bring our fondest best wishes to you and your mother for a beautiful Thanksgiving. How blessed we all are and how grateful we are each day just to see the sun come up.

Prudence, your letters always brighten my day, and please know how much we appreciate your writing even though we seem to be lacking in time these days. As I once told you, you are my link to Hawaii and your letters take me back to a land I have loved and hope to visit often. So please don't give up writing!

Also wanted to tell you that we have found a charming house on 72nd St. just off Lexington Ave...3 stories with an ample basement, garden, and room for domestic help. Nanny will continue to come in just for the day, and as you can imagine has become quite a devoted fixture.

Presumably we won't move in until well into the new year, but Lucy is so excited to be able to use some of the family pieces her mother has been urging her to take now. You'll have to come and see after we're settled...whenever that will be. So maybe make it sooner.

I'm being called, so shall bundle up lots of love from all of us as always and hope this finds you in the pink.

Devotedly,
Pete

P.S. Can't help telling you about the time Buzz and I were on the train and met this Italian man in the bar who kept raising his martini and saying, "Here's to allofus." So we'd respond in like, and then we realized he was toasting the olives! So here is to "allofus." Happy Thanksgiving!

Fondly,
Pete

Kauai
December 5th, 1953

Dear Pete and Lucy:

With all the Christmas music playing in every store you enter and the Salvation Army kettles ringing at the door, you can't help but slip into the Christmas spirit. Our Christmas festivities will include the ranch parties and we are so looking forward to having Sara and Alika with us for Christmas Eve dinner. They'll be with his family and plan to come back for the family's New Year's Eve party. Happy, happy!

Guess this will be your last Christmas in the apartment, and Len must be looking forward to Santa's visit, thereby bringing jolly old St. Nick and the childlike Christmas spirit into your lives. Next year at this time, the twins will be into the tissue paper and ribbons. Tradition is a wonderful thing, isn't it? Especially all the Christmas cards with pictures and notes, the raisins and nuts, the eggnog, the Christmas carols, the nativity scenes and more. May all the blessings of the true spirit of Christmas be with you and yours, my dear friends.

We've had some heavy rains that have washed down gulches and gullies but, thanks be, no loss of cattle. Consequently, riding up into the mountains has been curtailed for a while...Kua's orders.

Through the hospital I've met this charming young nurse, Nora Macdougal, about my age, and obviously from a very poor family in Scotland. Her brogue takes a bit of getting used to. Imagine coming from the highlands to answer a plea for more nurses. She was so grateful when I invited her to stay here until she finds suitable housing. Hopefully she'll be with us over the holidays and play the bagpipes for our carols. I should really make a tape of her talking with Kua with his Pidgin English. Sounds like foreign tongues. He tells her of the menehune and she goes him one better with their leprechauns. What a unique pair.

Mama is doing beautifully, and before dinner the three of us sit on the lanai for our cocktails, and she has been telling Nora of her girlhood on the ranch and how Hawaii was in her day. Of course, the dear girl is absolutely fascinated and this in turn prompts Mama to bring up more stories of the ranch! Most of the stories I'd never heard.

Wonder if you're having a white Christmas...enjoy whatever you have! Please know you and Lucy will be with us in spirit Christmas Eve at the children's service and at dinner. So cheers and aloha!!! From our house to your house...fondest love!!! Merrry Christmas!!!

And lest we forget..."Peace on earth...goodwill towards men!"

>With a heart full of love,
>Prudence

New York
December 15, 1953

Dearest Prudence:

Lucy is sitting at her desk madly addressing Christmas cards, the children are fast asleep and so I've taken to my desk to write you from the both of us. It's snowing outside, and I don't know why but it reminds me of the time a bunch of us decided to dig a pit and roast a piglet, Hawaiian style, at the fraternity house. It was a beautiful afternoon and after burying the porker, we retired indoors to imbibe in a few. Then a freak snow fell like a thick blanket and we couldn't locate the imu. Naturally, the little trotter finally ended up cooking in the oven.

Did Buzz ever tell you that story?

The twins are absolutely thriving. After their six pm feeding they're put in their playpen and so begins family bonding until their bedtime. It's so amusing to watch the interaction between Emily and Ian and their handling of toys. Of course, there was great excitement when Em's first tooth appeared. Len couldn't wait for me to come through the front door to tell me the news. The gurgling beauty is no longer toothless. My great-aunt Louisa sent silver teething rings from Georg Jensen's, but Emily much prefers the multicolored circle of plastic rings mother's cook sent. She's fascinated by all the colors and clutches it as if it's hers alone and leaves Ian with a silver ring. She'll learn!

We've persuaded the Hopkinsons to come in and spend the night at the Union Club Christmas Eve so they can be with us Christmas morning. This is a big concession on Grandpa Hopkinsons' part as he loves being in his own home at Christmas, but these grandees really have him under their spell. Of course, Lucy's mother is delighted to be out from under the responsibilities of Christmas Eve at home for once. This is truly breaking with tradition, so Lucy is working towards a festive Christmas Eve dinner and an exciting Christmas morning. Thank goodness the H.'s are early risers!

This year we'll have to skip going to Philadelphia for New Year's, obviously, but a few in for champagne and late supper should suffice. Lucy loves the holidays and I'm not sure with the move coming up whether she'll go all out on decorations as usual or not. Like Buzz, I'll put up the tree and the lights and that's it.

Your presents are hidden but will be the first to go under the tree dear Prudence. Will take photos so we can share our Christmas joys with you. I was so happy to hear that your mother is doing so well and you have that Scottish lassie with you. Good company for you, too. I guess girls wear kilts, too, don't they?

Well, my dear, pau for now. It's getting late and best we retire before the dawn comes up too soon.

So deck the halls, jingle dem bells and may the true spirit of Christmas find your heart at peace and your life full of love at this joyous season! What was it...Mele, mele ka leeki...you know what I mean...Merrrrrrry Christmas!!!!

With fondest love from "allofus"
Pete

Kauai
December 26th, 1953

Dear Pete:

1953 is slowly fading and before we welcome in 1954, just want to send greetings for a Happy New Year full of good health for all the Thornes, a successful move to the new home and joy and peace throughout the coming year with a big helping of love!

Our Christmas season was such a happy one, and there was so much going on and joy abounding that dear Mama never had time to shed a tear, at least in my presence. Christmas Eve dinner was so festive with Alika and Sara, Nora, the Scottish lass, the E.R. doc, Hal Faye, Mama's old friends Anna and Dan, and a few of the quilting ladies and their husbands who seemed a bit "hilahila"...uneasy... at first to accept, but they were a great addition actually. They told some hilarious stories from the past that had us all in gales of laughter. When Alika got up to make a toast, I thought this was the moment, but the dear boy looked at Mama with such devotion in his eyes then drank to her health...and most of us knew who else, too.

It's amazing, Pete, but I seem to feel a "new Mama" emerging...someone so much stronger in her faith and courage and so much surer of herself now, too. I detect a lot more pride in her Hawaiian blood and the old ways. After all, her roots go deep in Hawaii. While Papa was alive, I never saw her in a muumuu, but now she seems quite comfortable wearing them around the house in the morning. In the old days women had a muumuu for sleeping, one for morning wear at home, a silk one for evening and one for swimming. It was quite a sight the other day when she and the quilting ladies went swimming at their friend's secluded beach all wearing muumuu that billowed out like balloons behind them in the water and clung to their bodies as they emerged from the water desperately clutching the folds! Wish I'd taken a picture of their girlish modesty. Then the other day Nora stepped on a wana and the heel of her foot was a mass of black spines. Instead of suggesting a doctor Mama went out in the garden and returned with some laukahi leaves to make a poultice that she securely strapped on the area. The next morning that potent weed had drawn out all the black spikes. You can imagine Nora's surprise.

As a matter of fact, Grandma told me how she had stayed up one night applying fresh poultices of laukahi leaves on Grandpa's infected leg, which saved him from having it amputated. Mama told me later that Grandma was a great believer in the Hawaiian herbs and Hawaiian salt for healing, but, of course, today, one tends to overlook these natural remedies in favor of medicine from the doctor.

The other day Mama invited a few of her old friends in for lunch, and I wish you could have seen those dear girls thoroughly enjoying the Hawaiian kaukau Matsu specially prepared...raw fish, steaming laulau, lawalued mullet, sour poi, and every known condiment. Maybe they enjoyed it even more as they dispensed with silver in favor of their fingers and daintily dipped into each dish with grace and relish. What a difference from those formal luncheons in Honolulu.

I've finally bought a tape recorder and have it going at the cocktail hour. Mama's stories of her youth and tales of life on the ranch are fascinating. Between her stories and Kua's it would make for a wonderful story of old Hawaii.

Shall be thinking of you quaffing your champagne New Year's Eve. We'll be at the Paoa's for their fabled paina, and maybe some good news announcement! So here's a toast to 1954...with all good wishes and lots of love to all!!!!! God bless and thanks be for all our memories.

Love knows no distance in true friendship.

Happy New Year!

> Devotedly,
> Prudence

New York
December 31, 1953

Dear Prudence:

Happy New Year to you and your mother from all the Thornes!

It's going to be a great new year...I can just feel it. Lucy went all out with Christmas decorations and Santa was more than generous with each of us. Len can hardly contain herself and I'm swept up with all this joy and excitement and only hope I'm imparting some of it to you, my dear Prudence.

Interesting about the change in your mother. Are you sure there is no royal blood there? Had you thought of writing the story of old Hawaii yourself, my dear? She and Kua should be great inspirations just for starters.

Shall be thinking of you New Year's Eve and want a full report of the paina and who got the pig's tail.

Here's to 1954! Cheers!

All our love and affection,

As always,

Pete

Chapter III

Kauai
January 13th, 1954

Dear Pete:

Happy New Year!

Things are finally settling down after a joyous holiday season, topped off with the Paoa's celebration. Yes, the engagement was announced after the blessing of the food at dinner and you have never heard such cheering and toasting! Sara and Alika certainly didn't fool anyone. Such a divinely happy couple with so many people's blessing. They hope to be married sometime in May this year so we have some excitement to look forward to.

Nora had the best time of all of us over the holidays, especially New Year's Eve. We dropped her at the Paoa's house early that day as she desperately wanted to be there to watch Parker prepare the imu from start to finish...heating the rocks, placing the pig, fish, chicken, sweet potatoes, and bananas on the bed of banana and ti leaves spread over the coals. She even helped shovel dirt over the gunnysacks that covered it all. Then she helped Lei set and decorate the table with layers of ti leaves and even picked the flowers and fruit from the garden for the table decorations.

She was such a good sport at dinner, eating everything that was put before her...guess who got the pig's tail? Everyone loved her, and I think Scotland has lost a daughter. She tried so hard to sing along with the cowboys and when they sang, "Come on Nora, letta go your blouse," then began the lilting old Scotch hula, "From the Bonnie Banks of Scotland to the Shores of Waikiki came a little lassie," she adhered to custom and got right up to go through the hula motions with a Scottish twist that left us all convulsed with laughter. Too bad she wasn't wearing her kilts!

We couldn't help noticing Alika's brother, Hinano, who, with his big brown eyes framed in curling lashes, followed Nora's every movement and was being quite attentive. He's handsome with a great physique and is the physical ed teacher at the local high school.

Oh, and Nora is quite the artist, too, and has done some terrific sketches of Kua. Animation personified. Hopefully she'll let me send one off to you. She's found an ideal cottage not far from here and is happily settling in. I knew the Scotch were honest, hard-working people who watched their pennies, and now Nora has proven herself a true Scotsman, well loved by all. What a treasure she is besides being a good friend.

Have been spending a lot of time putting the tapes and stories of Mama's together, tedious work but at least we'll have a lot of it down. Maybe I should think about writing it up properly.

So here we go into a new year. Will be anxious to have

pictures of the new house when you're all moved in. Take care of your family and we'll keep in touch.

As always,
Prudence

New York
March 4th, 1954

Dear Prudence:

Being a mother of three active little ones is certainly a challenge but makes the days fly by so fast I hardly have time to catch up with myself. The moving process is even slower than I imagined it would be as there were considerable repairs to be made on the house which we thought be best done now rather than disrupt us later.

Pete has been in Washington for the past week and isn't sure when he will be home. We all miss him so much, especially in the evenings. With spring in the air we're trying to get out to walk in the park en famille, although it's not quite the same without him. Thanks be for nanny!

Now that we have a definite date for moving into the house, I'm targeting for the twins' birthday, June 12th, to spend the first night in our new home! Imagine a year ago that day we were sharing quite an experience, weren't we, Prudence, and I shall ever be grateful to you for your being so caring and kind that day. I've thought of it so often and feel so remiss that I haven't written you, but both Pete and I relish your letters and I'm always going to write you but never do. Please forgive.

Now I feel badly because I am writing for a particular reason and hope you will excuse my imposing on your good nature. Pete has talked so much about the wonderful Hawaiian food served for special occasions in the Islands that I wondered if we could plan a little Hawaiian feast to celebrate our first night in our new home on the 12th and the twins' first birthday.

What would be the simplest meal you could send safely from Kauai...I am open to suggestions and hope to be able to get some of it here at specialty shops. Also Pete loves the maile lei so maybe a few of those, ti leaves and whatever you think.

I remember going to a baby luau with Buzz to celebrate a child's first birthday. So hopefully you and I can plan something that would please and surprise Pete no end!

The twins are growing so fast. Crawling is their speed, but it's comical to see them try to stand on those sturdy little Hopkinson legs then plop down and begin all over again. They do so enjoy bath time, and I yearn for the day we can take them to the beach. Ian made great points by saying "DaDa" or the equivalent of!

Incidentally, Len calls "Tutu's" blanket her "gaga" and it's a magical maneuver to whisk it away to be washed!

Hopefully some day we'll get out to the Islands...just Pete and I for the first time, at least...and then as a family. Meanwhile, lots of love, dear Prudence from "allofus."

> *Fondly,*
> *Lucy*

P.S. I do hope I can keep the Hawaiian party a secret from Pete!!!

Kauai
April 2nd, 1954

Dearest Lucy,

We were overjoyed to hear all your good news...the plans for moving into the new house and the progress of the children. I'm sure the days are full with no time left over.

How dear of you to think of having something Hawaiian ! that would please Pete no end. I discussed it with Kua as he is the expert on such matters, and he began recounting all the good times he and Buzz shared with Pete and got carried away by your plans. You'll be safe in his hands so please don't give it another thought. We'd all love to be a part of such a happy celebration... double, really, or maybe it's a triple!

Kua's mind is made up. He and Hattie will be going East to see their grandson graduate from Colgate the end of May, so he wants nothing more than to go to New York and do the paina for you on the 12th. At this point I can see him taking over your kitchen and preparing a feast fit for the gods ! from the Mai Tais to the last crumb of coconut cake.

He will plan everything down to the last jar of poi, so relax and enjoy, if, of course you are amenable to this. Just let us know how many for dinner and he'll be in touch directly with you. Don't worry. It will be a Hawaiian menu that all can and will enjoy...no "whaaaat is that"?

Mama and I would love to send the lei and feel we are a part of the happy event, too. So count on us for the ti leaves, flowers, and lei. Kua plans to ship what he'll need from here and buy the rest in the city. As long as he can be in your kitchen at least by noon on the 12th.

Alika and Lucy will be getting married in Honolulu on May 30th, and Mama and I will go over early as we've been included in a few of the festivities. We plan to stay at the Halekulani for that week and the following week, and will have a party for them at the family-owned restaurant, The Willows, which does a superb job of private parties in a secluded corner of the rear garden. Mama and the matriarch of the family (who so lovingly planted all the foliage around the spring fed pond at the restaurant) became fast friends through their mutual love of plants. So it will be more or less like entertaining in our own home away from home.

Nora and I will be helping decorate St. Andrew's cathedral the day of the wedding. It's an old Hawaiian tradition that friends do the decorating at weddings, funerals, and parties. It's not considered work as everyone has such a good time visiting and doing what has to be done. The reception will be at the Carrington's Honolulu home.

Meanwhile we have the Kuhio Day rodeo coming up and will give you a full report.

Can't wait to see pictures of the house and a few capturing the excitement of the "housewarming party."

Lovingly,
Prudence

New York
May 1, 1954

Dear Prudence:

Couldn't be happier and more excited after receiving your enthusiastic letter!!! Have just written to Kua with all the details, and as you advise, am relaxing and ready to enjoy an unforgettable evening. Hawaii comes to New York! As a matter of fact, I suggested they stay at the Lexington Hotel, because I'm sure he'll be going to see the Hawaiian show there. Ray Kinney has been quite a drawing card.

Oh, Prudence, again you have come to my rescue and I love you all the more for your endearing friendship and especially for keeping in touch through all your beautiful letters. God bless.

Wish you were coming! Hopefully later. In the meantime, lots of love.

Devotedly,
Lucy

P.S. Obviously I couldn't contain myself and spilled the beans to Pete who couldn't be happier and can't wait to see his old pal Kua.

Kauai
May 20th, 1954

Dear Lucy and Pete:

Great excitement! Kua and Hattie took off yesterday for the East Coast with quite a bit of "Hawaiian luggage," cartons full of last-minute Hawaiiana for the party. Of course, he's shipping more to you directly. Then we are packed and ready to leave tomorrow for Honolulu.

Kua hasn't been back east since before the War, when he went with a group of music boys engaged to play at a wedding reception on Long Island. The family had spent a summer at the Royal Hawaiian Hotel and become quite attached to several of the beach boys and fell in love with Hawaiian music. At the last minute one of the boys couldn't make the trip, so Kua was called to fill in and he gladly accepted. I remember his coming back to the ranch and telling me about the night they were playing and kept seeing little lights flitting through the trees. Of course, they were fireflies!

Anyway, he's kept in touch with the son and will visit them in New Canaan.

The flowers and lei should be arriving a day or so before

the 12th, the lei need to be refrigerated, and immerse the orchids in water for quite a while to revive them. Just keep the ti leaves damp.

Oh, how Mama and I wish we could be two places at once! But we will be with you in spirit.

The Kuhio Day rodeo was a rousing success and we even had cowboys from Hawaii and Maui competing, which livened things up around the island. Kua was in his element, grinning from ear to ear when he presented your trophy to one of our own cowboys' sons. As you can well imagine, once the competition was over and the stress and strain gone, the party that followed was a rollicking affair, so Mama and I just faded away quietly so they could all feel free to "lettagotheblouse"!

The weather has been simply glorious and spring is here with all the orange day lilies and gardenias bursting forth in all their glory...just as St. Luke described. And, of course, the black-breasted plover, kolea, are gathering by flocks to fly back to Alaska on the appointed day. They arrived here thin but fatten up considerably to make the long journey home. Since they don't have web feet, only the strong survive the long, nonstop flight between Hawaii and Alaska.

Know we'll be with you in spirit!

Affectionately,
Prudence

New York
10 June 1954

Miss Prudence Farnham
Kauai Hawaii

Kua Hattie flowers all here in great shape   STOP   Happy
Island-style reunion   STOP   You're certainly with us in spirit
STOP   Mahalo and Aloha   STOP

Lucy and Pete

Kauai
Hawaii
12 June 1954

Hopkinsons
72nd Ave
New York NY

Thinking of you all in new home   STOP   May it be a place of
comfort a haven of peace where all will always feel secure
STOP   Our fondest love   STOP

Prudence and Laura Farnham

New York
June 13, 1954

Dear, dear Prudence:

Before I do anything else today, I want to write you while the
birthday/housewarming party is still so fresh in my mind and to
tell you how much we've been thinking of you. The twins were
on their best behavior during the cocktail hour and safely

launched into the "Terrible Twos." Len wore her lei like a true kamaaina and was rather reluctant to leave for bed when we went in to dinner, but we certainly were proud of the children.

Kua was the hit of the evening after we coaxed him out of the kitchen. When he took up his ukulele and sang a few tunes and then Hattie did a hula – the party was made!

Oh, Prudence, it brought back so many, many memories of my days in the Islands with the Farnham family...tender memories that made me yearn to return. I am once again convinced that there is nothing quite like the true Hawaiian spirit with its warmth, caring, and giving nature...from the heart, not monetarily.

Lucy couldn't believe all that Kua brought and then found in New York City. It was a true Hawaiian feast from start to finish and, as you promised, not a dish was sniffed at. He did a suckling pig in the oven that could have come directly from the imu, the chicken done with spinach and coconut milk tasted the same as luau leaves, and where he found the salt salmon for the lomi salmon is still a mystery. It all came back to me and how well I remember preparing these dishes under his supervision so long ago. Somehow he managed to find some appropriate crabs at the local fishery, and the haupia pudding he made was sheer nectar.

As soon as our respective parents, Lucy's sister and her husband, and two other couples who we are very fond of arrived, we followed Kua and Hattie through each room as they sprinkled water mixed with Hawaiian salt they had brought and chanted a few prayers in both Hawaiian and English which were very touching and I detected a tear on my mother's cheek. We feel the house is properly blessed and what a memorable evening!!!

The house is truly all we had hoped for and more. I know we'll be spending a lot of time in the garden this summer and so you know what I'll be doing...back to the earth. Lucy did a fantastic job on the interior, decorating with her good taste and quite a few pieces from her mother. It's comfortable, livable, and family-oriented. You must come and see!

The maile lei you and your mother sent are now draped over the grandfather's clock in the entry hall and the aroma permeates the room.

So back to reality now that I've imparted my deepest gratitude to you for all you did to make the party such a happy success.

Fondly,
Pete

New York
June 15th, 1954

Prudence, dear:

Oh, how blessed Pete and I are to have your friendship and Kua's undying devotion!!! If anyone could have put me more at ease and more relaxed in my own home the day of a party, it was that dear, sweet Kua! How he created the miracles he did, I will never know, but all the extra help reported they wished all their "bosses" were as kind and considerate.

After the twins woke up from their afternoon nap, Pete, Nanny, Miss Crowe, Kua, and Hattie joined us for the birthday cake and ice cream with Len. Safely tucked in their highchairs, they attacked the ice cream and cake with both hands and, of course, you know who blew out the candles for them! Then the three of them were dressed for the party...Len looked adorable in her muumuu, Prudence, and the twins had on their best bib and tucker.

Kua's beautiful delivery of the prayers was absolutely touching, and we feel so blessed in our new home. Pete and I know

*that we could never ever repay him and Hattie for all they did
for us, but Pete did promise him that as soon as possible we'd
be out to see you all on Kauai, and you know how Pete is
about keeping his promises!!!*

*So, dear Prudence, we share so much, I just had to share
this joy with you, too. Our gratitude and happiness know no
bounds.*

*Have a wonderful summer and we'll send pictures as soon as
possible.*

*Devotedly,
Lucy*

Kauai
June 23rd, 1954

Dearest Pete and Lucy:

Mama and I couldn't have been happier to receive your
enthusiastic letters and to hear how well everything went.
We knew the paina would be top notch! On their return,
Hattie and Kua couldn't wait to tell us all about the house,
the garden, the children, the blessing, the party, your parents...oh, we sat on the lanai entranced by their glowing report. Actually, I think the visit with you overshadowed their
grandson's graduation.

They have piqued my curiosity to the nth and will have to
come east to see for myself, and what a happy reunion
that will be.

Sara was a radiant bride, and I did have to smile when I
saw Alika's face light up so reverently when he saw her approaching the altar on her father's arm. Later, they danced
down the maile-bedecked aisle on wings of love. Hinano was
a handsome but nervous best man, but, thankfully, through

Nora's sparkling personality, he became more relaxed at the reception, especially on the dance floor.

Quite frankly, I was a bit apprehensive of Mr. Carrington's facial expressions as he had put up a slight fuss when he realized the affair between Sara and Alika was reaching serious proportions, but I was so relieved and happy to see him escorting Mrs. Carrington down the aisle after the bride and groom with the widest and proudest grin on his face. And well he might be proud of this part-Hawaiian son-in-law who will take such good care of his daughter.

Because Mama knew that Parker and Lei were quite nervous and shy about going to Honolulu and being with Sara's family and all the Honoluluans, she had them stay at the Halekulani Hotel with us. She needn't have worried, they made such a handsome couple and rose to the occasion beautifully...naturally. His toast to the bride and groom was very touching in its simplicity and sincerity. Of course, Nora and Hinano enjoyed every minute of the reception and fell quite naturally into the romantic spirit of the evening.

According to all the flattering notes and phone calls after the party we gave for the young at the Willows, I can honestly say the Hausten family out-did themselves. Mama asked a few of Hattie and Parker's Honolulu relatives and several of Buzz and Alika's mutual friends, besides the Carrington family and the bridal party. As it turned out, Parker's brother had served in the legislature when Mr. Carrington was governor. Everyone gathered round the pit when the pig was taken out of the imu and I'm sure Mrs. Hausten personally supervised the food as it was all perfectly delicious. Quite a few toasts made for a festive evening.

I must admit, though, I kept thinking of Buzz and missed him so. I don't know when I've thought of him so longingly as during all the festivities, but I know he was with us in spirit and think Sara felt it, too. She and Alika have rented a charming house in Nuuanu valley and eventually will buy something I'm sure. He seems happy to be practicing in Honolulu, but wonder if the lure of an outside island will prove more attractive later on. You know the adage about not taking the country out of the boy.

While we were in Honolulu we went to see a polo game, but, alas, it wasn't the same brand that you and Buzz played by a long shot. It was at night and held at the local stadium so you can imagine how confining it was...horses galloping down the field and then being reined in for a sudden stop on the sidelines. There weren't any automobiles, no tooting of horns, and frankly, the players themselves weren't all that glamorous!

So now we can truthfully say that after two weeks in Honolulu, we are more than ready to settle back into ranch life. Actually, I'm anxious to continue writing up all the notes I took on Mama's stories.

Nora applied and was able to transfer to the west side Waimea Hospital, closer to the ranch, which makes more sense. Mama regrets not insisting Nora stay in one of the guest cottages here, but it's better this way. The romance seems to be past the budding stage.

At one point while reading your letter, I suggested a trip East to Mama, but there wasn't even a spark. I think her passionate love of Hawaii is causing her to relax comfortably back into the Island style of living each day and enjoying all God's blessings.

Anxiously awaiting pictures.

Fondest love,
Prudence

New York
July 27, 1954

Prudence, dear:

Today I picked up the prints we had made for our families
and you so am sending them off post haste. Also I wanted to tell
you how sad I felt for you missing Buzz at the wedding. I can
understand so well and yet, we must be grateful that Sara found
someone so compatible to love, cherish, and honor. I'm sure
that the two of them realize the fundamental bond that brought
them together originally, and you may even have gained a
sister. I agree with you about the "country out of the boy" and
today with the return of so many service doctors into the civilian
medical slots and all the changes in medicine, I wouldn't be
surprised if both Alika and Sara give serious thoughts to moving
to an outside island.

Family doctors who made house calls any time of the day
or night are a fading race. You know, I was so interested to
hear Kua telling me about Parker's role as the ranch doctor.
As a matter of fact, he reminded me that Parker had treated
me for an eel bite, of all things, when Buzz and I were fishing
on the reef with a glass box. Stupid malihini stuck his finger
into a hole to see if the fish was still there. He was, but a very
long and vicious one!

Parker, a skillful polo player, was probably Buzz's ideal
and may be responsible for his choosing medicine. And now
his son is a doctor, too. How proud he must be of Alika, and
yes, I can imagine their popularity at the wedding. Oh Prudence, I too, miss Buzz on so many occasions and just talk
to him, and so whenever you feel you want to discuss something with him, just write me...your big brother, remember!

The garden is taking shape...thanks to flowering shrubs
and potted plants from the nursery, and we're out there a
good part of the daylight hours. I have my eye on a perfect

spot for an imu. We adore the house and Lucy has made it a loving home.

And, Prudence, I urge you to write down your mother's memoirs. I know it will take discipline and hard work, but don't be discouraged ! just keep writing. When you think it is ready for a critique, I will be only too happy to do so and be honest with you. I might even be able to find a publisher here in New York who would be interested in publishing a book of the Islands, as Hawaii seems to be "the destination point" today.

Well, dear girl, keep well and writing. Have a gainful summer and fondest love as always to you and your dear mother.

Devotedly,
Pete

Kauai
August 17th, 1954

Dearest Lucy and Pete:

The pictures arrived and they certainly tell the whole story!!! Oh, the children are so adorable, you both look so well, and the house and the garden!!! We can see how happy you are to be in it, and you'll never feel the depressing heat of New York in that lovely garden spot. We sat on the lanai and slowly went through the generous bunch of pictures and can't thank you enough for sending them so we could share your joyous day. I'm so glad you included the ones of the twins in their christening dresses. Imagine their having been worn by both families for so many generations back. They must be exquisite pieces of museum quality with all the tiny pleats and ivory buttons and rare lace.

Well, I'm writing, Pete, and it does take discipline but I'm finding it all so interesting and can't wait to get back to it every morning for several hours. Kua had hopes that I would take over as ranch manager so he could retire, but after conferring with Mama we decided to train one of the promising young men who was born on the ranch. He's devoted to Kua and the ranch and am sure that when Kua does retire, Kawika will bring modern changes to the ranch that will be so beneficial...not that Kua isn't doing a magnificent job now, but times are changing.

Sara and Alika came over for a visit with his family and were able to spend some time with us, too. Sara and I had some lovely rides, and yes, Pete, she and I have so much in common and are truly devoted to one another for which I am most grateful. I treasure our friendship. Alika didn't think Parker was looking too well, unfortunately, and found him rather pakiki, or stubborn, to the idea of going to Honolulu for tests. He seems fine to me, but then I'm not a doctor, and hope there is no cause for concern.

An old friend in Honolulu has asked me to be in her wedding in mid-November, which will be fun. I will be seeing many of our old school friends who'll be coming out from the East for the wedding. Unfortunately, I haven't been able to talk Mama into coming with me, so I'll stay with Alika and Sara who will be in the wedding too. It will be a treat for me to be with them in their own home.

All well here and hope the same with you. Hugs and kisses all around, and we haven't really stopped going through the pictures yet!

> Fondest love,
> Prudence

New York
September 5, 1954

Prudence, dear:

Can you, believe...Miss Len was off to preschool today. Excitement galore! Unfortunately, the only sad note was that she had to leave her beloved gaga at home...I just had to write you this!!!

We had such a happy summer in the garden and Pete really enjoyed working at improving it. The ladies of the Garden Club are eyeing it for a house tour so hope he keeps up the good work. The apple tree has even produced.

Some friends of ours, Dick and Haley Daley, are going to be on Kauai sometime in October, and if you're not off to the wedding I think you might enjoy meeting them. They tried to talk us into going with them but Pete took his vacation this summer so that was that for another year!

We go through the pictures of the housewarming still, too, and each time we discover something new. The twins are walking now and I try to be patient in disciplining them about interesting objects on the coffee tables, but then I never know which one did what!

We love hearing from you, Prudence, and Pete is so pleased that you are writing. He can't wait to read it. Please send our fondest love to your mother and heaps to you, dear girl.

Fondest love,
Lucy

P.S. Still can't believe our good fortune...we've found the most reliable young lady who comes with the highest recommendations to be our live-in help. She is marvelous with the children and loves to cook! We are so blessed!

Kauai
October 9th, 1954

Dear Lucy and Pete:

How grateful I am for your bringing me together with the Haleys! What a perfectly delightful couple, and how fortunate for me that we had mutual friends in Asa and Ginger Caldwell of Honolulu, who invited us to their divine retreat on the Big Island. Oh, how we thought of you and wished you could have been with us!

When we arrived on Hawaii, the Caldwells met us at the small Upolo Point airport where the runway is so short it makes landing a rather frightening experience. Thankfully, the plane stopped short of the ocean below. We piled into a truck and drove through charming rolling green hills, dotted with cattle, then headed down through dry ranch land to Kawaihae harbor, crowded with freighters and small craft, to board Asa's sleek Chris-Craft. His wiry little handyman, Fuji, followed in a slower speedboat with our luggage and fresh supplies. As we zipped along the barren Kona coast line, I could just imagine the steam created by the hot lava flowing into the sea. We passed very few sandy beaches and one resort. The winds picked up and we continued a wet and bumpy ride past miles of black lava. Asa finally slowed down when a group of houses appeared and beached the craft so that we could safely jump out onto the beach. Then Asa took the boat offshore to anchor and swam in.

Soon Fuji beached the smaller boat further up on the sand, unloaded our bags and supplies then he sped back to Kawaihae where he lived.

What a spot! The main house is nestled in a coconut grove beside a pond full of fish, and down by the beach are several guest cottages. The only way to reach this hideaway is by boat, and there is neither electricity nor phone, only a large storage tank for water, a generator and tanks of gas. Imagine bringing in all the household furnishings by boat, not to mention building materials! We were doubly appreciative when we realized just how much work the Caldwells had to do preparing for our visit. The logistics sure take planning.

We had three glorious days of relaxing, trips down the coast to swim and picnic in remote bays, and always ended up the day in a deep, crystal clear pool in the lava that was fed by very cold spring water. Oh, I just can't describe it all to you.

One morning, Asa's Uncle Lot and his handyman Paulo came roaring in on his super-charged speedboat to pay us a visit, bearing wriggling lobsters that Paulo grilled for our lunch. He is one of the most fascinating, handsome, elderly gentlemen I have met in a long time...a true native son of Hawaii. Dressed in faded palaka shorts, an old tee shirt and fishermen's reef shoes, he was still handsome with a very distinguished appearance. I was thrilled that he had such fond memories of Mama and playing polo with Papa and Buzz. He wanted to know if Granny was alive and he wants to come and see Mama.

We had a most enjoyable afternoon talking story with this charmer and as we walked him down to his boat, he looked up and out to sea and announced that the weather was changing and no way could we get out by boat the next day as planned. The alternative was to walk along the King's Trail through miles of black lava to his place on the Kona coast just past Puako.

He swam out to the boat, Paulo hoisted him in, turned and waved us goodbye, gunned the motor and took off almost above the water. Asa smiled and said, "Typical Uncle Lot. My mother calls him "Rascal," her lovable kolohe brother, and as you heard, he's awfully proud of being the great-grandson of one of Hawaii's high chiefs."

The next morning his predictions were all too true. The winds came up and the sea was choppy...no way could we get out by boat. So we relaxed, ate a hearty breakfast, put on our walking shoes and hats and started hiking across the desolate ancient lava flow. After three hours of marching under a broiling sun, we reached his compound and there he was in the cookhouse waiting for us. There were steaks and squabs on the grill, mullet from the ponds frying, and a pot of rice and bowls of poi were ready on the table set for six. He was such a gracious host, urging us to relax and forget about leaving and stay, but alas, we had planes to catch. He had Paulo and another man drive us across the lava on a bumpy road to Kawaihae.

On the way to the airport, Asa explained that Uncle Lot had moved to Santa Barbara when he married a very prominent local socialite. However, his love of the Islands kept luring him back to his property on Hawaii and his wife would have none of the Island living. Then on each visit he began building his various houses around the ponds that dotted the lava beds and along the water's edge. No one was surprised when he divorced his wife and returned to the Islands to enjoy his "kanaka-style" living. As you can imagine, he never lacks for company.

The Haleys will describe the visit much better with all their photos and home movies. Do you remember Asa at Princeton about your time, Pete? It was fun for me showing the Haleys Kauai, but compared to this 4-star experience, just another "run-of-the-mill touristo bit." Incidentally, Fuji retrieved our luggage the next day and shipped it home to us. He certainly is a priceless gem.

The only sad note here on the ranch is that tests and x-rays discovered a small tumor on Parker's brain, and an operation is scheduled for November first. Alika finally persuaded his father to go to Honolulu with him for the tests, which Parker did rather reluctantly, but being a doctor himself, Parker knew Alika was right to suggest the precautionary trip.

Naturally, Lei is beside herself with worry, as is the whole ranch family, but we keep positive thoughts. She admits that Parker had been complaining of headaches lately, but not to the extreme that they must have been. She will be staying with Alika and Sara in Honolulu for the duration of the operation and recuperation, and Mama is helping to organize a group to hold a prayer vigil for Parker on the day of the operation. Between these people there is strong mana, or divine power, that will help Lei tremendously ! and after all, Parker is still a vigorous and youthful 72-year old!

For some reason Kua seems reluctant to turn the management over to Kawika. Something about his not being satisfied with Kawika's history of business experience in Honolulu. Of course, this is very important, but I hope things will work out.

Sorry to end on a grim note, but I'm sure all will go well. Fondest love to all of you and will keep in touch.

Devotedly,
Prudence

New York
October 25, 1954

Dearest Prudence:

Lucy and I are distressed to hear of Parker's impending operation, but thank goodness he listened to Alika. Is there anything we can do here? Do they need financial help? Please advise me, as I would love to help if we can.

The Haleys came for dinner and after going through all the

pictures and seeing their movies, they painted us green with envy. Maybe I should renew my friendship with old Asa. I played tackle against his guard at college.

Have been able to get away for a long weekend so Lucy and I will be off to Bermuda for R & R sometime in late Nov. or early Dec. The Hopkinsons will hold down the fort. The twins will keep them busy and amused!

Wanted to get this in the mail as quickly as possible and shall be thinking of you all Nov. first.

Fondly,
Pete

Kauai
2 November 1954

Mr. Peter Thorne
400 East 72nd St.
New York, NY

Doctors pleased with successful operation   STOP   Lei grateful to their skills prayer group and your offer   STOP   Will be in touch   STOP   Enjoy R & R   STOP

Prudence

New York
November 18, 1954

Dear Prudence:

Just wanted to thank you for the reassuring wire. However, please let me know if they are ever in need financially or he needs further treatment. I'm on the board at Sloan-Kettering here in the city and consider it the top cancer center.

Lucy is packing our duds as we leave for Bermuda tomorrow and am I ready for it...she is, too. With the holidays coming up she'll need to recharge her batteries for the big push she always seems to exert to make things festive and bright.

Please remember me to the Paoas and have fun at your wedding in Honolulu.

As always,
Pete

Kauai
November 20th, 1954

Dear Pete and Lucy:

Hope the Bermuda jaunt brought the roses back to your cheeks!

Back home to catch up on the ranch news after all the festivities surrounding the wedding in Honolulu. However, being with Sara and Alika was really the frosting on the cake. Oh, so rewarding to be in a home with so much obvious love and devotion. Sara and I were like teenagers at the pre-nuptial parties, and Alika, bless his heart, did his best to produce eligible young doctors, but no sparks ensued! I think the wedding was a blessing after all the suspense and worry over Parker. He and Lei are home taking it pretty easy. She's so smart, she bought him a sturdy tank and filled it with water and colorful fish for him to watch and care for. He's even named a few of the fish.

Nora had been rather coy but finally admitted that she and Hinano have decided to be married during the holidays, when he'll be on break from school, rather than wait until summer. Though it's hard to believe, she's been here a year so due to leave. Maybe Parker's illness made them aware of how precious time is and how life can shift so quickly.

Everyone is thrilled for them both, and Mama has offered to have the wedding here at the ranch house as you never know about the weather at that time of year.

Maybe you wonder how I'm reacting to all this romance around me...but I'm happy. I see quite a bit of Hal Faye but nothing serious. Life is good, especially now that I am devoting more time to writing the story of the ranch with renewed interest and ambition.

Grandma has emerged as such a strong and vital character. Raised on the original ranch and dominated by a doting but strict father, she was first and foremost a born horsewoman. Her mother was reputed to be related to King Lunalilo and she spoke Hawaiian almost exclusively. After her father died and Grandpa had bought the ranch, she became more involved with running the ranch and a staunch supporter of Grandpa. Wasn't he the lucky one. At least her devotion to the ranch was eclipsed long enough for her to have Mama and enjoy her moopuna. Her love of horses and riding are the basis of so many stories.

Grandma loved Mah-Jongg! It's the one pleasure she'd give time to and enjoyed playing with the wives of the Chinese storekeepers and laundrymen in the village. From what Mama tells me, she gave those shrewd women keen competition ! and didn't mind taking their money!

How can I ever record all these stories ! her foibles, beliefs and tales ! some reckless and daring. She wasn't an ehu Hawaiian for naught! I wonder if Grandpa ever really tamed her.

Governor King and his wife were here with us for the night when he came for a political rally. We did so enjoy having them, and I do believe he has solved Kua's doubts about Kawika. After the governor saw him, he kept wondering where he had seen him. It really bothered him until he remembered and took Kua aside. It seems Kawika was working as a clerk in one of the senator's offices during a session of the legislature and became seriously involved in a bribe scandal but it could never be proven in court. However, he left Honolulu under a cloud and went to the mainland before returning to Kauai.

Always straight to the point, Kua faced him with the facts and Kawika seemed relieved after admitting the fraud. His departure has raised questions, naturally, but for the sake of his father, who has been a faithful blacksmith on the ranch most of his life, Kua has told no one but Mama and me and written the governor a letter of gratitude. Mama knows this will go no further.

Athalie Loomis had written Mama that she would be in Honolulu for a Garden Club annual meeting and would love to come to Kauai for a few days afterwards. Of course, Mama answered immediately and she'll be with us for Thanksgiving. Poor dear, I do hope she won't be exhausted from all the entertaining those ladies of the Honolulu Garden Club are famous for. However, she can relax by riding with Kua et al.

Can't believe Thanksgiving is upon us! We've asked John and Robert to come here for Thanksgiving dinner as we all have so much to be thankful for. It will be a real Hawaiian celebration, or hoolaulea. We wanted a festive board with Athalie Loomis, the newlyweds, the soon-to-be-weds, Lei and Parker, and quite a few others. Mama is inclined to make the dinner menu a real hapa-haole feast with more Hawaiian dishes ! to the point of dispensing with mashed potatoes and gravy, for goodness sakes! She wants both the turkey and pig to be done in the imu with assorted island produce. She wanted a coconut cake, but I won out for good old pumpkin and minced pies!

So you see, life is not dull around here. Mama enjoys life more and more each day.

Have a blessed Thanksgiving and God bless you all.

Devotedly,
Prudence

New York
November 25, 1954

Dear Prudence:

Greetings from "allofus" for a joyous Thanksgiving!

Grateful for your newsy letter, and the remarkable recovery of Parker. If you ever think they need financial help with medical bills, please let me know.

How fortunate that the governor recognized Kawika, and I commend Kua for handling the unfortunate situation so tactfully.

The weather is turning nippy, the twins are more and more inquisitive and Em emerges as the more aggressive of the two. Len loves school but is always in a hurry to be home with the twins.

Our R and R in Bermuda was perfect. The weather cooperated until the last day. We woke up to rain on the roof and decided to stay in bed and order breakfast in the room. We felt we owed ourselves a lazy day after all the tennis, bicycling, and swimming.

So now Lucy has re-charged her batteries and is ready to chair the Junior League's charity ball at the height of the holiday season. Maybe we'll win a trip to Hawaii. Right now she's concentrating on Thanksgiving dinner, as my family is coming and the Carringtons will come in for the noon meal. If all goes well, the twins will be ensconced in their highchairs to add a bit of informality and distraction.

Oh, Prudence, we are so blessed! My precious family is my life...thank God!

Delighted to hear that you'll be having a gala Hawaiian Thanksgiving surrounded by devoted family and friends...I like what I see. Please send them all our aloha.

Blessings and fondest love,
Pete

Kauai
December 19th, 1954

Dear Lucy and Pete:

Have waited till the last minute to send the special Christmas cheer and best wishes so as to be able to tell you about Nora's wedding. I do hope this reaches you in time because it brings lots of love!

She and Hinano planned a perfect wedding, down to the last detail, so as to share their happiness with the ranch families and a few from the hospital and school staffs. It was a very simple and romantic celebration.

Nora was a radiant bride in a simple white holoku with a short train. Crowning that gorgeous red hair was a crown of colorful flowers and she carried strands of pikake lei. Hinano was handsome in the traditional Hawaiian formal attire for men of a white shirt, open at the neck, and white pants, with a scarlet silk cummerbund wound around his waist, the fringed ends hanging at his side. The sash belonged to his grandfather, who had worn it at informal luau given by King Kalakaua. They were both barefoot.

We couldn't have asked for a more perfect afternoon for a wedding at the beach. Kua probably put out a hefty shot of gin, with ti leaves, to appease the rain gods. We all gathered at the rambling ranch beach house and then followed the bride and groom to the beach where the minister was waiting. With the setting sun sparkling on the crested waves as a heavenly background, he performed a very meaningful ceremony with a Hawaiian blessing. One touching moment was in the middle of the ceremony where Hinano stepped back, picked up his guitar, looked into Nora's eyes and sang one of the old beloved Hawaiian love songs. There wasn't a dry eye in the house!

Once the minister pronounced them man and wife, the felicitations and kissing had been done, and tears of joy wiped, we all followed them into the big reception rooms that had been transformed into a veritable garden of greens. One table held assorted homemade pot-luck pupu and another dispensed beer and champagne, the latter Mama's gift to make the occasion extra festive.

The sumptuous luau was served on the covered lanai with many toasts for happiness. Then a wire from Nora's parents was read. I know you'll appreciate the "detail"! Yep, the crispy, curly tail of the pig was tied with a white satin ribbon and presented to the bride, who shared it with her groom! We all cheered and remembered back a year ago when Nora had been rewarded with the tail.

After all the feasting, we ambled back down to the torch-lit beach with a full moon on the water and relaxed on the fine makaloa mats to listen to the music. The impromptu hula dancing ended with Parker dancing a charming, slow hula to an old Hawaiian love song with Nora. Where else but in Hawaii!

Then the happy couple changed into riding clothes and rode off on horseback down the beach. The next day they went by Jeep over a gap in the mountain to spend a week at Hale Kipa, the secluded spot bordered by cliffs and ocean so ideal for honeymoons. As a grateful patient of

Nora's during his stint in the hospital, Henry endowed her with the rare gift of the stay in appreciation of her TLC. Not many people outside of the family are that fortunate.

Between the wedding and the ranch Christmas parties, Mama and I will just have a few in for dinner after church Christmas Eve, including her old friends and Hal Faye, then we'll spend the following day quietly at home. Sara and Alika will be with Sara's family for Christmas and Lei, wisely, is being quiet. Parker's recovery is miraculous and he does take things easy...under the watchful eye of Lei. He never ceases to express his appreciation and thanks to everyone who saw him through his ordeal ! especially the prayer group. But their New Year's Eve party is out of the question. Mama is thinking of having "open house" New Year's Eve, which might be fun.

Not having heard from you, I gather that you did not win the grand prize at the ball. Keep trying!

My heart rejoices to think of the two of you, Len, Ian, and Em all together awaiting Santa! I'm sure that old St. Nick will spend a little extra time at your house and enjoy the cookies Len, no doubt, has helped the twins put forth. Yes, my dears, the blessings of family and friends at this time of year, especially, are so doubly important and fill our lives with exultation in the highest.

So this brings ever so much love and best wishes for a blessed and merry, merry, merry Christmas with continued blessings throughout the year. And so we rejoice! Hugs and kisses all around.

Affectionately,
Prudence

New York
December 24, 1954

Dearest Prudence:

Santa is waiting in the wings, Lucy is still decorating the house, and the children are beside themselves with excitement! I think I've covered the present situation, thanks to Schwarz and Cartier. Lucy is so hard to shop for but I think she'll like the Hawaiian-style bracelet engraved with her name you helped me find.

This year we'll concentrate on Christmas Eve dinner and plan to have the Carringtons, my sister and her husband, and a few close friends who don't have family. This way we can devote Christmas morning entirely to the children and the tree. The Carringtons will spend the night at his club.

It's been snowing and I keep thinking of you out there in paradise with Santa coming in a canoe and swimming on Christmas Day! The yearning for the Islands is always pulling me back!

We'll be here quietly for New Year's Eve unless something comes up the last minute, but being on a weekend gives us more precious time to be with the children and do things together.

We'll be thinking of you all over the holidays and know that your days will be full of love and devotion. Some day we would love to be able to bring the children to your Christmas Eve service at the little church. Enclosed is a check for the offering that day.

So, dear Prudence, another Christmas, another new year on the horizon and I look forward to our continuing correspondence, for which I am so grateful in so many ways.

Lucy joins me...she's still at the cards...in sending fondest love to you and your mother. Our prayers go with you now and forever more. God Bless. Merry, merry Christmas! We'll be thinking of you!

Fondest love as always,
Pete

Chapter IV

Kauai
January 12th, 1955

Dearest Lucy and Pete:

Happy New Year!!!

Hope your holidays were as joyous and fulfilling as ours. I thought of you all Christmas morning and hope Santa emptied a full bag!

Christmas was very quiet so Mama did decide to have the open house on New Year's day, and people dropped by between 5:00 and 8:00. I couldn't believe my eyes when I spotted a familiar face I couldn't quite place coming up the lanai steps, and it turned out to be Uncle Lot, looking dapper all dressed up in a blue suit, bearing ilima lei for Mama, followed by a group of musicians. He isn't one to do things in a small way!

If you only could have seen Mama's expression when she saw him! They embraced like two old sweethearts, and he apologized for coming uninvited but was on the island for a golf tournament and couldn't resist coming to see us. As the crowd thinned out, he and Mama sat out on the lanai and talked about the old days and their youth while the musicians serenaded them softly in the background. To say Mama was overjoyed to see him is the understatement of the New Year.

He finally left about eleven o'clock but not before making us promise that we would come to see him soon. I wasn't surprised when Mama readily accepted. It was fun listening to Kua and Uncle Lot talking story about their polo playing days at Kapiolani Park in Honolulu and the celebrations later.

Parker is doing beautifully and the doctors in Honolulu are amazed, but very pleased over his progress. At least a little hair has grown back. Lei has been the model of patience, as it isn't easy keeping a good man down.

Nora and Hinano are sublimely happy settling into their new cottage they were able to find closer to the ranch. She's anxious to learn the Hawaiian language and with that Scottish brogue it will be interesting.

Between the wedding and the spirit of Christmas, Hal has become quite attentive and romantic! He is a dear person and great companion but I don't know whether I'm ready for this...and is he, really? Time will tell. Don't hold your breath.

His mother is here visiting him and I do have to laugh at times. As you probably know, growing up in Hawaii we were never conscious of anyone "being Jewish" and I was always envious of some of my best friends having seven days of Christmas. I must admit it was a shock to me when I went East. Anyway, Mrs. Faye is the typical doting mother with all her fussing, food preparations, and questions. However, she's a good sport and Hal is so patient with her. Sometimes I wonder if she came out of sheer curiosity to see

who Hal had been mentioning too often and why, maybe.
Anyway, it's been fun showing her the island.

So we're into the new year with great expectations. Hope
you'll be coming this way sometime during the year! In the
meantime lots of love to you both and hugs and kisses for
the children.

Fondly,
Prudence

New York
January 28th, 1955

Dearest Prudence:

Happy New Year and here's to an eventful new year!!!!
*We had a lovely, relaxing Christmas even though the twins
were into everything! Len woke us early Christmas morning
and climbed into our bed to open her stocking, and then she allowed us to get up so we could gather up the twins and go down
to the tree in time to greet my parents.*

*The colored blocks you sent Em and Ian keep them amused
by the hour... perhaps they're budding engineers and architects? Len is entranced with her doll, which reminds me so
much of the one I had as a child...even to the tatting on the
petticoat and underwear. Wherever did you find such an exquisite doll? She's named her Missy.*

*Unfortunately, my mother has a broken hip due to a fall at
the Colony Club where we had just finished lunch. Thankfully
the doctor was able to see her immediately and she is resting
comfortably in the hospital here in the city. Dad is staying at
the Union Club but goes home occasionally, which mother
keeps urging him to do, as he isn't used to sitting around a
hospital room.*

I'm sorry for the broken hip, but it's wonderful having mother so near me. I'll miss her when she goes home with a nurse in two weeks. However I'll be home more. I don't know why I seem to be so tired in the evenings.

Pete's beginning the new year with a pretty tough case and has to spend a lot of extra time on it, but it means a feather in his cap if they win. Otherwise he's in good spirits. He was so amused reading your description of Uncle Lot's unexpected arrival and remembers him during polo season as a great sportsman and a dashing cavalier. He wanted me to say "hi" when I wrote. How nice for your mother to renew an old friendship.

Looking out at the falling snow, I wish we were all in Hawaii right now for some of your sunshine. Hope this finds you all well and, I'm sure, busy. I do wish we knew Hal Faye. Keep us posted!

Lots of love, dear Prudence.

> *Devotedly,*
> *Lucy*

Kauai
March 1st, 1955

Dear Lucy and Pete:

Seems ages since I last wrote but have been busy...delightfully so! Mama and I, along with Kua and Hattie, flew to Hawaii as guests of Uncle Lot. There are certain spots along that Kona shoreline that are inaccessible except by boat, but what heavenly spots. Having stopped there briefly recently I knew what to expect, but Mama was overwhelmed.

He outdid himself with warm hospitality beginning at the airport, where he met us with lei, until our last farewell. I felt much safer landing at the airport in Waimea, which is a bit more civilized than the Upolo Point airport, and the view down the mountain to Kona is spectacular. We stopped for lunch at the town's best Chinese restaurant. Obviously he was one of their best customers, famous for his generous tips, as everyone bowed and scurried around, taking drink orders then presenting food fit for the gods.

After all that food, we felt more like taking a nap than riding down the winding road to Kawaihae harbor to board our host's shining Chris-Craft. Once safely aboard, Uncle Lot maneuvered the boat slowly out of the busy harbor, turned, saw that we were all holding on for dear life and gunned the engine for a half hour's bumpy ride I skimming above the waves.

When he finally slowed down, we could see signs of civilization—tall coconut trees and a few houses that seemed to sprout from the lava. This was Uncle Lot's private domain. Approaching the pier, Paulo tossed us towels to dry off. Mama had the ride of her life and loved every minute.

His place is incredible – miles from anyone – so it spreads out considerably. It is quite different from Asa's in that there is no beach. Uncle Lot has created a comfortable compound on the old lava flow with numerous ponds, some filled with mullet and others strictly for swimming – and is the water cold. His screened-in sleeping house is isolated on a little island in the middle of the biggest pond, with a narrow path over the lava connecting it to land where the central meeting house is located. The comfortable big room with inviting hikiee opens on to a lanai right on the water's edge. The cook house and dining area are nearby, but set back.

Mama and I shared a comfortable two-bedroom cottage on the water, adjacent to the one where Kua and Hattie were. It was heavenly. Uncle Lot made us feel so at home and we just relaxed and enjoyed all the attention and three meals a day cooked and served beautifully. You were never out of earshot of the crashing waves against the lava coastline and we never left the property.

One day we piled into his old Jeep and bumped our way over the lava up to the back of his property which he referred to as his "mauka forty." Here were all the chicken and squab coops, pigpens, and guinea hens' reserve. No wonder we ate so well! Beyond that are houses for all the help.

Uncle Lot provides yukata muumuu for the ladies and kimonos for the gents. One day when Uncle Lot was out fishing, Mama just couldn't resist stepping down into the cold water and swimming around with her billowing muumuu behind her. Frolicking like a child, she was enjoying herself until she heard the Chris-Craft approaching. It was a sight to see her clambering out, giggling like a school girl, and once again frantically pulling the clinging muumuu from her body.

Uncle Lot spends the day in his old palaka shorts, t-shirt, and his fisherman's tabis, but in the evenings he is nattily dressed in trousers and aloha shirts made especially for him from Musashiya's in Honolulu. After cocktails on the lanai, watching fiery sunsets and an occasional green flash, dinner is served in the cook house by candle light.

He and Kua had some great fishing offshore, and so we feasted on all kinds of seafood. I could see where Mama was enjoying every bit of what Uncle Lot refers to as his "kanaka-style life." We were there a week, perfectly happy with a lazy routine of climbing down the ladder on the pier to swim in the ocean, the ponds, and just sitting on the lanai reading, chatting, or sleeping. I do believe Mama was lulled by the romantic Hawaiian atmosphere! She never even picked up her knitting once.

Meanwhile, back to reality, Kua has resigned himself to just staying on as manager of the ranch as he hasn't been able to find the right man. Parker is doing beautifully and says his recovery is due to prayers and the Hawaiian herbs his family has provided as a tonic. Alika flies over whenever he can get a day off just to check on him. He and Sara are still happy in the rented house and don't seem to be in any hurry to buy anything. He seems quite satisfied with his practice in Honolulu.

Going back to Uncle Lot. I wouldn't be surprised if he wasn't very quietly pursuing Mama!!! He is such a lovable man and always so thoughtful. Mama had a fresh lei every morning and another in the evening. I think she rather fancies a man's attention after her years of widowhood but I certainly wouldn't let on to her! We'll just see how it progresses, but Mama is almost kittenish. Kua and Hattie seem amused and happy about it, too.

As for me, Hal and I had a quiet dinner in town recently and discussed our future and I just had to tell him that I wasn't quite ready for any real commitment and he confessed he hadn't actually made up his mind about remaining in the Islands. I really wish I felt more in love with him, but somehow there doesn't seem to be any flame on my part to fan. He's good company, honest, hard working and certainly perseveres, but I don't want to break his heart. So now that we know where we stand we can continue a lovely friendship.

Now I'm really concentrating daily on the ranch story and it seems to be jelling.

Next month is the rodeo and wish you were coming out to present your cup. It will be an Island-wide invitational rodeo, which should bring some life into the island. Guess who's coming with the gang from the Parker Ranch? Yep, Uncle Lot.

Think of you so often and hope everyone is thriving and well.

Fondest love to each of you.

As always,
Prudence

New York
March 11, 1955

Dearest Prudence:

Was just wondering if you would be in New York next September? It's just that I may need your moral support! Yes I'm delighted over the idea of being pregnant again, though Dr. Harriman takes a dim view of this. Of course, Pete is delighted but we haven't mentioned it to Len as yet...time enough.

However, as happy as I am over the turn of events, I must admit I've been feeling simply dreadful recently and have had to cancel out on quite a few commitments and plans for Easter vacation which is irritating but sensible. I don't remember ever being this sick before.

But enough of me. Your letters always bring such happy news and you must know how much Pete and I enjoy hearing from you. What romantic news of your mother! I guess we can't expect such a handsome woman to spend the rest of her days knitting. I do think that if I weren't pregnant Pete and I might fly out for the rodeo...and to see Uncle Lot and Hal!

We're delighted the story of the ranch, which you are devoting so much time to, is coming along so well. Maybe, when you come East in the fall, you can see a publisher.

The twins are growing so fast and it's interesting to watch Em take the lead in everything. Ian seems content to go happily along.

We look forward to being in the garden again as Pete has taken such an interest in the planting and tending of the garden beds, too. It's fun working together.

Dull letter but told Pete I wanted you to be one of the first to know since we shared so much at a critical time in my life.

So lots of love from us all, dear Prudence, and we'll be in touch.

> *Devotedly,*
> *Lucy*

New York
March 30, 1955

Dearest Prudence:

Lucy tells me she's written you about the coming "blessed event" and of her happiness, and we would both love it if you could come East in September. However, I know I can be absolutely frank with you. Confidentially, I am not at all sure she should be having this child after talking it over with Dr. Harriman. He certainly doesn't want to upset Lucy, but has asked me to keep an eagle eye on her, especially when she is prone to go overboard on activities. Tennis, especially.

I give you my word this turn of events came as rather a surprise to both of us, but as you know, Lucy has always wanted a large family. The twins are quite a handful, really, but Lucy seems to take them in her stride. We can talk more about September as time goes on, but Lucy is sincere in wanting you here, and, of course, you know how I feel!

There has been more pressure on me to move to Washington, but, of course, now it is impossible even though it would mean a big promotion for me with so many perquisites. Thankfully, my superior is an understanding fellow. I haven't even mentioned it to Lucy as I wouldn't want her to feel responsible for my not going.

How I wish we could be out in the Islands for the rodeo, but it looks as though we won't get out there for at least another year now, for which I am truly sorry. All I can say, Prudence, is that your letters mean so much. They keep the Islands alive for me.

Please remember me to your dear mother. I do hope Uncle Lot is sincere in his courtship! I'm all for it!!!

> Lots of love to you, dear Prudence,
> Pete

Kauai
April 16th, 1955

Dearest Lucy and Pete:

What exciting news about your being hapai, Lucy! Mama and I are thrilled for all of you. Of course, I'd love nothing better than to be with you again in New York in September or whenever is best. How dear of you to even think of me. Having never had the blessing of motherhood, you may think me rather free with advice, Lucy, but all I have to say is please take care of yourself and don't overdo. Your and the baby's health comes first, so rest when you can. I'll be interested to know Len's reaction to the news, but am sure she will anticipate having another sibling with great joy.

The ranch story seems to be falling in place naturally, but still lots of work to do. I doubt I could finish it by September, but maybe it would be an incentive to do so if I thought I could see a publisher...wouldn't that be exciting.

In the meantime Kua and I are concentrating on setting up some guidelines for hiring the next manager. When this is done, I would like very much to send you a draft, Pete, for any suggestions or corrections, as I value your professional scrutiny and advice. It is essential that we hire the right man for this important position.

The rodeo was a huge success, and Lochanvar is riding off with his princess. Yes, the romance seems to be progressing. Uncle Lot was a perfect houseguest, and when he heard I was writing the story of the ranch, he had quite a few tales of his own to add, especially about our polo ponies. One evening Kua was on the lanai having cocktails with us and they began talking about the polo playing days. I was thrilled for another angle and quickly set the tape recorder down quietly. So between Uncle Lot and Kua I think I have some colorful material. It was too funny. There was

Uncle Lot holding a skein of wool for Mama to rewind and trying to use his hands to regale us with his stories! Every once in a while I do sense that years ago Grandma kept an eagle eye on this handsome young gallant whenever he hove into sight!

Your trophy was won by a young, aspiring cowboy from Parker Ranch who has his heart set on becoming a pro on the mainland circuit. So now Uncle Lot wants to donate a trophy in Sam Parker's name, the founder of the vast Parker Ranch.

It was a most exciting day, even though we were hot and dusty most of the time. The boys from Waimea were distinguished by the fragrant maile lei on their cowboy hats, and several from the Ulupalakua Ranch on Maui sported rose lei, their island's flower. The boys from Oahu really outdid us all and wore yellow tee shirts with "Oahu" emblazoned in black on the back and black Stetsons with ilima lei. It was really quite a festive affair...dust and all.

The celebration later was a cowboy's idea of a really "letta-go-your-blouse" party...lots of beer, pupu, stories, and music. We could see that Uncle Lot was reveling in exchanging stories with the cowboys who felt so at ease with him. So Mama, Hattie, and I left quietly. It's amazing how Uncle Lot seems to fit in so naturally with any and all types of people. The cowboys' wives and girlfriends were kept busy serving up the food and keeping libations cool, but I am sure they retired early, too.

Ever since Uncle Lot asked Mama to come to a house party he's having for some of their mutual kamaaina friends next month, she speaks and plans for little else. I've never seen her so animated and wonder if the turn of events will start arousing the other guests' curiosity in June.

Easter seems late this year. After decorating the

graves the day before, we helped the ladies dye Easter eggs for the combined ranch/church children's egg hunt, an annual affair held after church down at the ranch beach place. From dawn to dusk, Easter was glorious, both spiritually and weather-wise, and the egg hunt/picnic was well attended. Mama loved all the ohana being together.

Lucy, I do hope you will soon be over the "draggy days" and feeling yourself again. I shall keep you in my prayers and look forward to being with you!

Fondly,
Prudence

New York
April 26, 1955

Dearest Prudence:

Of course, I will be delighted and only too happy to go over the papers you and Kua draw up for guidelines for the new manager. With your permission I would transfer your thoughts into legal language for your and Kua's approval of any corrections or additions. Then, if you would okay it and return the papers to me, I can formally draw them up for you and Kua to sign and the deed will be done.

Lucy just doesn't seem to be her old self, tired all the time, no enthusiasm, and wants to sleep a lot. At least she isn't asking for watermelon at midnight. She talks of having a birthday party for the twins in June but doesn't really seem to have her heart in it.

She asked me to please send her love and will write soon, but don't count on it. Truthfully, Prudence, I don't know what to say about planning on coming East in September if she continues to be so lackadaisical. Maybe a visit after the baby is born – maybe even October would be better. Then you could keep her from post-natal blues and we could all relax and enjoy you. Anyway, I toss this out for you to think about and hope you don't mind my being so frank.

Keep us posted on the romance. All I can say is that Uncle Lot would be a very lucky man to win your mother's hand!

In haste but with love..

As always,
Pete

Kauai
May 14th, 1955

Dear Lucy and Pete:

Exciting news! Mama and Uncle Lot will be married here on the lanai June 25th!!! I wasn't at all surprised when Mama called from Hawaii to say she was staying on for several days after the party. Finally she called to tell me when she'd be home, but when I met the plane there was Mama with Uncle Lot beaming from ear to ear. He said he had come to ask me for Laura's hand.

He stayed for a few days while they told me their plans, which sound ideal. They want to divide their time between Puako and the ranch and do some traveling...so many exciting plans. Don't you love it? I'm so happy for them both and wanted to share the news with you, too.

Just as well they only want the immediate families at the wedding, otherwise heaven knows where the guest list would end. They plan to leave for Honolulu that afternoon and fly to San Francisco the next day with no other plans in mind. Ah, romance!

How we wish you both could be here for the happy occasion, but, Lucy, please take care, and I'm ready to come to New York any time...just let me know when!

Meanwhile lots of love and I'll keep in touch.

Fondly,
Prudence

P.S. In all the excitement, Pete, I forgot to say that Kua and I are most grateful for your legal advice and will do as you suggest. What a dear friend you are.

New York
20 May 1955

Mrs. Laura Farnham
Kauai Territory of Hawaii

Thrilled with the exciting news   STOP   Hope you'll be coming east on your honeymoon   STOP   Since we can't be at your wedding would love to meet Uncle Lot and do something for you here   STOP   Pictures please   STOP

Fondest Aloha,
Lucy and Pete

New York
May 27th, 1955

Dearest Prudence:

Pete and I received the dearest letter from your mother. It fairly bubbled over with romance and happiness. Isn't it wonderful to think that at their age they can start out anew and enjoy an exciting life together. I have been urging Pete to go out for the wedding as your mother reiterated how she had always thought of him as a second son. I wish I could convince him that I'd be fine if he took just a few days off and flew out. Goodness knows he flies around for the firm, and this is something he would dearly love to do, I know!

He's been so concerned over my condition, but I've been quite well lately, actually. Miss Mary is so capable, and the children are devoted to her. So this has been a big help, but I do try to spend a lot of time with them. We have told Lenny about the coming event and as you can imagine is thrilled. She keeps telling the twins how they're going to have a little baby to play with. She is quite the little mother!

It will be good to have you here, Prudence, but I hate to tie you down as the actual date isn't really firm yet and Dr. Harriman isn't sure, but it might possibly be a cesarean. So maybe we should plan on October...then you and I can go on a shopping spree for clothes...stopping long enough for lunch at my favorite haunts, which, incidentally, I haven't been to for quite some time. It would be much more exciting if you came then, now that I think of it...something for me to look forward to!

Back to your mother's letter. The one thing she is sad about is leaving you alone on the ranch, but they hope to spend some time there off and on to keep in touch. She realizes what a blessing Lot has been in her life and recounted so many little things he does to please her and make her happy. She's looking forward to many years of happiness with this man. How we wish we could meet him.

What on earth do you give such a couple for a wedding present!

Little Miss Lenny just came in and wants me to be sure and send you "lots and lots" of love...she has such fond memories of you.

Well, my dear, I'm all for Pete's going to Kauai, so I'll see what I can do. Meanwhile, "lots and lots" of love.

Fondly,
Lucy

Kauai
June 3rd, 1955

Dearest Lucy:

Loved hearing from you and know how much it would mean to Mama to have Pete...and you...at the wedding, but she understands the circumstances completely.

There's enough boxes and tissue paper in her bedroom already but still the boxes arrive from Magnin's...it's like Christmas. She says she doesn't want to spend any time shopping and being away from Uncle Lot in San Francisco. She'll have quite a trousseau when she's finished, but I think she has decided to wear a simple holoku for the ceremony and change into this stunning pearl gray suit, which just arrived, when they leave.

The ceremony will take place at 11 o'clock on the lanai and the bishop himself is coming from Honolulu to officiate at the service. After the ceremony, we will enjoy a leisurely lunch so they can take a five o'clock plane for Honolulu. They'll overnight at the Halekulani hotel and fly out the next morning for San Francisco.

Things are really buzzing around here. The wedding will be small...around 30 including Uncle Lot's sister and husband, their children, and a few of his favorite "calabash cousins," Kua and Hattie, Sue and Alika, the Paoas, and a few of Mama's close friends. Uncle Lot and Mama are planning a reception for the ohana on the ranch after they return from their trip.

Hattie and Kua have offered to do the floral arrangements in the house and concentrate on the lanai with maile
and large containers of white ginger. It will be a very informal gathering around the bishop as they say their vows.

Mama insists on planning the menu, which I'm sure will
include lots of champagne if Uncle Lot has anything to say
about it.

It's all very exciting, Lucy, and such happiness prevails.
Because of this and in the essence of time, I must ask you
to please do me a favor and tell Pete that Kua and I have
finished the paperwork on the profile and are sending it
along today. I'm so grateful for his help.

It was so good to hear from you, Lucy, and October
sounds like a perfect time...the fall colors and a "girlie
shopping spree!" So count on me. In the meantime, take
care of yourself and give everyone a big hug for me. As soon
as the pictures of the wedding are developed I'll send them
along to you.

Devotedly,
Prudence

P.S. Hope the twin's birthday presents arrive on time and
will be thinking of you on the 12th.

New York
June 8, 1955

Dearest Prudence:

The final papers have all been worked on and are here on
my desk. They seem to be in good order and only need your
signature. You two have done a fine job of defining just the

man capable of taking over the management of the ranch. I sincerely hope that you will find that man to carry on Kua's good work.

Lucy seems ever so much better. As a matter of fact, we took Lenny to Greenwich for the weekend and Lucy seemed so happy to be there with her parents and seeing a few old friends. I was very encouraged.

She has really been urging me to go out for the wedding and how I would love nothing better. I am going to look into this new non-stop flight United Airlines is inaugurating from New York to Honolulu. If I think Lucy is really doing well, I may just be aboard a flight the last minute and be on the lanai with you all on the 25th. But, naturally, it all depends on Lucy and whether I feel right about leaving her for a few days.

In the meantime the papers will go out in today's mail.

We finally found a wedding present for the bride and groom...no easy task! It's a handsome Steuben fish we hope might be right for Puako.

We were all greatly encouraged when Lucy organized an afternoon birthday party for eight little ones in the garden. A few of the mothers Lucy knew well were a great help and of course, Lenny led the troops in games. I even took the afternoon off to enjoy the fun, too. Lucy had asked her parents to stay for dinner, but we ended up having cocktails and dinner around her tucked into bed...exhausted.

Lots of love, dear Prudence, and am sure the excitement is mounting.

As always,
Pete

Kauai Territory of Hawaii
2 June 1955

Pete Thorne
72nd St
New York New York

Papers arrived today   STOP   Kua and I most grateful for
the legal wording and finished work   STOP   Wish you
and Lucy coming   STOP

Aloha,
Prudence

New York
23 June 1955

Prudence Farnham
Kauai
Territory of Hawaii

Flying United direct Honolulu 24th   STOP   Overnight
Honolulu   STOP   Will be on lanai by 11am 25th   STOP   Lucy
Lenny to Greenwich   STOP   All happy   STOP

Aloha,
Pete

Kauai
June 26th 1955

Lucy, dear:

   It's 9 pm and I've just returned to an empty house after
dropping off Pete, Sue, and Alika at the airport. Of course,

Pete will be home with all the news long before this reaches you but I'm so exhilarated that I have to talk to someone! It's been quite a day.

First let me say that Mama and Uncle Lot and I are so grateful to you, Lucy, for being such a good sport and urging Pete to come out. I do hope you were rewarded with a blissful visit with your family and old pals.

We couldn't have asked for a more beautiful day. Uncle Lot insisted on accepting Kua and Hattie's invitation to spend last night with them so Mama and I had a lovely relaxing breakfast together in her room this morning. She was so calm you would have thought I was the bride! She didn't even go downstairs to see to any last minute instructions as she felt secure in having planned it all so well that there wouldn't be a hitch...and there wasn't.

One of the ranch hands did the airport pick-ups so Pete, the bishop, Sue, and Alika all arrived early at the house, but I was ready for them. Uncle Lot's family had hired their own car and found their way soon thereafter. Alicia Caldwell is a charmer like her brother and reminds me somewhat of Mama...gracious with a great sense of humor. It was so good to see Pete! First thing he did was deliver your love to me and then later to Mama, so you were with us in spirit.

Mama was absolutely radiant in her silvery silk brocade holoku with a slight train. She wore graduated strands of pikake le,i reaching to her knees, and a small wreath of them in her hair.

Uncle Lot was so handsome in a dark blue suit, white shirt, red tie, and maile lei. I couldn't help shedding a few tears when I saw his expression as he came up the lanai steps and saw Mama. I think he had a few tears, too. They approached the Bishop together and we all gathered around them as the bishop began the ceremony. Looking right into one another's eyes, they repeated their vows very clearly with great conviction.

We all broke out into spontaneous cheers when the bishop pronounced them man and wife and urged Uncle Lot to kiss the bride. The girls appeared immediately with trays of icy champagne as we closed in to kiss and congratulate the beaming couple. When I kissed Uncle Lot, he whispered, "Thank you, dear. I'll take good care of her, and we'll be here whenever you need us."

I'm only sorry I didn't get more time to talk to Pete then, but I made sure that Mama seated me next to him at lunch. He was so pleased to catch up with Asa Caldwell. Seems as though everyone had something special to say as they raised their glasses in touching toasts that were received so graciously. You would have been so proud of Pete. When he got up, clanked his glass, lifted it, looked right into Mama's eyes and said, "Here's to my Hawaii mother who is responsible for my falling in love with Hawaii and feeling like one of the Farnham family. I'm only sorry Lucy can't be here with me to wish you and Uncle Lot all the joy and love we feel in our hearts for you, but thanks be to her urging, I'm here to meet Uncle Lot and know that my hanai Mama is in good hands." Mama was so touched she kept smiling and wiping away the tears.

Incidentally, the lunch Mama planned was delicious, but interrupted by many toasts. Hattie made and decorated the cake with white icing and a yellow ilima lei entwined with green maile. When they cut the cake, the music boys played the Hayward family's song, a beautiful love song, and in ac-cordance with tradition, Alicia and Asa rose to acknowl-edge the rendition.

It all went too quickly and before we knew it it was time for Mama to go upstairs and change. As they went arm and arm down the lanai steps, we threw plumeria blossoms at them and the music boys played a rousing tune.

As the car pulled away from the porte cochere and started down the driveway, we all stood waiting for the sound of the tin cans to clang. Henry, the driver, reported the couple thought it all in fun but had him stop to remove the rope of cans. But I do think they appreciated the prank, and it made them feel young and frivolous!

The rest of us all sat around visiting for quite some time, digesting it all. Uncle Lot's family will be here for a week so I look forward to showing them the island and getting to know Alicia especially.

By six o'clock everyone was gone except Sue and Alika, Pete, Kua, and Hattie so we relaxed on the lanai and snacked on leftover pupu and a real drink. We'd all had had our fill of the bubbly hours ago and were still full from lunch.

We couldn't be happier that you are feeling so much better, Lucy, otherwise I know Pete would never have come, but we did miss you. As soon as you can, I hope you and Pete will come for a real visit. I hated to see him go so soon and we didn't talk about half the things I wanted to. He took to Alika right away and hopes they'll go East some time so the four of you can do New York.

Pete was happy to be here, but I sensed that he was also anxious to get back to you. He was the proud father showing us the few pictures of the children he brought with him. You are so blessed, Lucy.

The house is so quiet after all the day's activities. So best I end this prattling and check on things before I try to settle down and get some sleep.

Many thanks again, dear Lucy, for lending an ear and encouraging Pete to come.

Fondly,
Prudence

Aboard United flight to New York
June 26, 1955

Dear Prudence:

Here it is, almost midnight (six a.m. in New York) the cabin lights have been dimmed, and most of the passengers are snoozing or trying to, but after such an exciting and memorable day I find sleep hard to come by! Oh, Prudence, how grateful I am to Lucy for urging me to come out. I'm only sorry she couldn't share in that happy day.

Lot is such a fine, distinguished gentleman with a merry twinkle in his eyes, and I know for certain that he will take good care of your mother, who obviously absolutely adores him. I know he will make up for all the sadness in her life. I hope I was able to talk him into coming East so that Lucy can meet him.

And how wonderful to see you again, Prudence! The view from the lanai is still as I remember it, thankfully, with only the forests of lehua trees, lush valleys and ocean below with not a house in sight. Being on that lanai was like coming home and going back in time. I'd forgotten what a big responsibility the ranch is and hope that you will find the right man to fill Kua's shoes.

You made the all too short visit flawless and relaxing...even to having presents for the children, which I never would have gotten around to doing. My only regret is that I didn't get in a swim, but then I couldn't have possibly done everything. Once Lucy recovers from this birth, we'll be out for sure. She deserves a beautiful trip.

The man across the aisle is eyeing me...guess my reading light bothers him, so shall take the hint and wind this up. Everything was just perfect, Prudence, and please let me know news of the newlyweds. I'll always be interested.

> Devotedly,
> Pete

New York
July 7th, 1955

Dearest Prudence:

Between your detailed girlie letter and Pete's version of the wedding, I feel as though I might have been there. He was ecstatic over everything, especially Lot. He couldn't say enough good things about him and I am most anxious to meet him...preferably not in this uncomfortable state.

The twins were thrilled with all your books! Ian is fascinated with the colorful pictures of the tales of Lono and his canoe and Em loves the story of the little Hawaiian twins. Of course, Lenny is only too happy to read to them. The muumuu fits her perfectly.

What with all the wedding plans, you were so dear to take the time to find such appropriate gifts. Maybe in a few years the twins can write their own thanks.

Am enclosing pictures of the children in the outfits you sent from Hawaii at the birthday party. They were thrilled and want to know when they are going to see Tutu and Aunt Prudence so they can go to the beach!

How I wish we were at the beach right now. It is so hot in New York, but the garden is a little respite, especially in the evenings. My parents keep urging me to come out to Greenwich for a week and I am sorely tempted, believe me, but the logistics of moving the troops is a bit overwhelming. If Pete keeps urging me to go, I just might...just to get away from the oppression of the city. However, the last few days in Greenwich was utter bliss...just relaxed and enjoyed.

This baby is so active and although I feel fine, it gets rather uncomfortable at times and especially at night while I'm sleeping...or trying to. Dr. Harriman sets the date around Sept. 15th...and then our shopping spree!!! I so look forward to our being together again, Prudence.

In the meantime, take good care of yourself...and what has happened to your friend, Hal Faye? I'll see who I can line up here for your arrival so it won't be too dull.

Lots of love as always. Pete said to say hi, too.

> *Fondly,*
> *Lucy*

Kauai
July 16th, 1955

Dearest Lucy and Pete:

The pictures with your good letter, Lucy, have just arrived and I'm so happy to have them. Trite but true... "how they've grown"!!! And please tell them that I'll take them swimming whenever they come out and visit me. Emily is the image of you, Lucy, the blond curls will serve her in good stead in the future.

Last I heard from the bride and groom they were enjoying being back on Hawaii and relaxing after their whirlwind trip to San Francisco, Pebble Beach, and Newport Beach. Mama said their friends couldn't have been more hospitable and kind but they were happy to have stayed at clubs and hotels instead of being houseguests. I guess, after all, newlyweds!

I've really had time to concentrate on the story of the ranch and am enjoying every minute of it. There's a lot of research to be done on the original ranch, and I keep finding all sorts of interesting facts in the old files. Mama's father was really a very cagey, but fair, negotiator. I'm trying to include inserts from his diaries, in which he tells of arriving on Kauai and riding around the island on horseback to immerse himself in the life by accepting the Hawaiians' generous hospitality and becoming one of the family for a spell.

The Hawaiians loved him. It was they who nicknamed him Kauka. He may have been a young Yankee from the West, but he fell in love with Hawaii, learned the language, lived among the natives, listened to their stories, helped them with their problems, and seems to have been a father image. Because of his rapport with the Hawaiians, he was able to amass his collection of stone artifacts found on ranch land.

Eventually, when Hawaiians became desperate for cash, they came to him with their calabashes, feather lei, or fine mats to sell. He paid them a high price because he regretted their parting with family heirlooms. When they offered him land, he was more than generous.

All the while he was looking for land where he could settle down and begin his life's dream of having his own ranch. Of course, he finally accomplished this, and Grandma was the final rewarding asset. A beautiful young Hawaiian girl who came from an old family on Kauai. Their romance would fill a book in itself.

Hopefully, you'll be able to get out to Greenwich for a little change of scenery, Lucy. If only the children were older I would love to have them come and spend some time with me here. It gets pretty lonesome at times rattling around in this big house. However, Hal is still in touch and we do share some fun times together but sense we both know that it will never lead to anything serious.

There really wasn't a let-down after the wedding, as the Caldwells were still here and it was a pleasure showing them the island and having them on the ranch. One afternoon, when the others were out sailing, Alicia and I had a quiet visit on the lanai. I learned more about her family than Uncle Lot ever told.

Her grandfather, a part-Hawaiian man married to a lovely girl from England, owned a vast ranch on the island of Hawaii, extending from the slopes of an extinct volcano down to the seashore. I gather from her tales that her grandparents really enjoyed the finer things of life and were famous hosts at the ranch, but loved to travel, too. Their daughter, Kapua, Alicia and Lot's mother, moved to Connecticut to live after she married. But she and Uncle Lot always loved to visit their grandparents on Hawaii and felt more at home in Hawaii than in the East.

Alicia met her husband in the East while both in school, fell in love, and eventually they were married. It didn't take them long to move to Honolulu, where he is a stockbroker, and they have their own retreat on family land in the mountains of Waimea, where she loves to go. The ranch land has dwindled, as pieces of the valuable ocean-side property are being leased to developers for resorts, which Alicia isn't too happy about. The ranch managers are trying to keep a cap on the height.

I could see she was devoted to her brother and so happy that he had finally married his one true love. Uncle Lot was 21 when he fell in love with Mama, who was 18. Their romance blossomed and they made a handsome couple. At one point, they even thought of eloping. Alicia had never seen him so happy. However, Grandma thought Mama too young to have such a serious relationship. She considered Lot an irresponsible playboy spoiled by a doting grandmother, so she took Mama on a round the world cruise. Lot was heartbroken, but eventually his roving eye met an attractive Santa Barbara girl, and they soon eloped. After the glamour of the Islands wore off, she decided Hawaii and Lot were not for her and so they were divorced. He went through two other marriages that failed. He never married again.

Their Grandma had left her vast estate in trust to Lot and Alicia, so he was able to concentrate on improving his land on Hawaii.

His meeting me at Asa's and hearing of Mama kindled his suppressed love for her. He was older and wiser so gradually won back Mama, who had always had a special place in her heart for her first love.

We both agreed he can still be a rascal but he will always love Mama and see to her happiness.

This brings ever so much love to all of you and am looking forward to being with you in the fall.

> Devotedly,
> Prudence

New York
July 27, 1955

Dear Prudence:

Lucy and the children are in Greenwich for a few weeks, and I've just returned from spending a happy weekend with them. The Hopkinsons enjoy having them all there and are dauntless in my book! From early morning to lunch they "roll with the punches" and show great patience with all the activities, questions, and utter disruption of their daily routine. However, their ritual of afternoon naps seems to rejuvenate them. Lucy is thriving on all the pampering, good food, and being with her old friends.

However, now that I am back home after an active weekend and battling traffic into the city, the house seems so quiet. Although I should be thinking of retiring, I thought I'd relax a bit by sharing our news with you.

The twins love Granny's pool and are learning to swim, but we really have to keep an eye on them, especially when Granny is doing her laps. Lenny now wants us to call her Lani, after reading one of the books you sent. To tell the truth, it's an easy transition.

We seem to be busier than ever at the office, but they are very considerate about keeping me close to New York for now.

Sorry the "honeymooners" didn't get east, but had the warmest letter from the bride expressing such appreciation for my being at the wedding and thanking us for the fish. She sounds ecstatic.

Hope you're concentrating on your story. I've talked to a publisher friend of mine, so we're all just waiting.

> Fondly,
> Pete

Greenwich
August 3, 1955

Dearest Prudence:

It's joyous being here with Mummy and old "Pops," and the children are reveling in being outdoors, especially exploring the forest on the property and discovering the joys a pool can bring! Mummy found an excellent swimming instructor who comes every morning to "blow bubbles" with the twins, and their progress is fantastic. It's really quite comical watching them trying to show off their prowess in the water. Em, the leader, is the braver of the two, but Ian, the shadow, eventually dares to follow even though it means coming up gasping for breath.

I'm feeling well and have to watch the scales what with Mummy's cook who's been here since I was a child and knows what I love. The other day she looked at me intently and announced it is certainly a boy as I'm carrying him so high. Either sex, we'll all welcome the new baby.

Lenny wants to tell you something so shall enclose her note.

She has so many playmates her age living nearby...one even has a life-size dollhouse...that the twins actually miss her.
Another two months and we'll have our shopping spree!
Until then, dear Prudence...

> *Fondest love as always,*
> *Lucy*

Dearest Aunt Prudence:

Thank you for sending the book about Lani and her friends in Hawaii. I love the pictures. Now I want to be called Lani, too. Ian calls me "Yani." Hope we go see you next year.

> I love you,
> Lani

Kauai
August 17th, 1955
Dear Lani:

Thank you, thank you, or mahalo, for your beautiful letter. You write so well. I'm thrilled to think you love the name Lani and want to be called that, too.

You all seem to be having a happy time with Grandma and Grandpa and hope you are taking good care of Mommy.

It's so exciting about the new baby, and I can't wait to see all of you in New York soon after it is born.

One of our mares just had a handsome golden colt, and wish you were here to watch her try to steady herself on her wobbly, long legs. Some day I'll show you around the ranch and get you and the twins on horses.

Please give Mommy a big hug...gently...for me and tell her I'll be writing soon.

Aloha (love),
Aunt Prudence

New York
19 August 1955

Prudence Farnham
Kauai
Territory of Hawaii

Have lost Lucy and our son   STOP   Devastated   STOP
Hopkinsons here with children   STOP

Pete

Kauai
Territory of Hawaii
20 August 1955

Peter Thorne
72nd Ave
New York, N.Y.

Your grief is my grief   STOP   My compassion and sense of loss deep   STOP   My love and prayers surround you and children   STOP   Would fly to be with you if any help at all STOP   Everyone here saddened   STOP

Love,
Prudence

Kauai
August 20th, 1955

Dear Lani, Em, and Ian:

Even though there are thousands of miles of ocean and land between us, I am with you and Daddy in my prayers. We are all sad that Mummy went to sleep and woke up in another world...apart from us in a land called heaven. I like to think of her in a beautiful sunny room where she can look out and see a garden overflowing with beautiful flowers of every color. When she steps outside, many, many little children come running up to her to ask about you, her most favorite and special of all children.

She'll tell them what precious little children you are, especially what good swimmers you are, Ian and Em, and how many little friends you have, Lani. Then they'll want to know all about you...what you like to eat, your favorite stories, do you have coloring books and a favorite toy? can you blow soap bubbles? and do you have any pets? and much more.

She'll answer all their questions and tell them how she has left you with a loving father knowing what a good life you will have together.

Yes, we shall all miss Mummy, but she never really leaves us. She's up in heaven watching over us and knows when to touch our hearts to remind us she loves us.

Take care of Daddy and give one another big hugs and kisses for me. I love you very much.

Aloha,

Aunt Prudence

New York
August 21, 1955

Prudence Farnham
Kauai, Territory of Hawaii

Services set for Lucy and Brett 4 pm August 24 St.
Matthews New York   STOP   My family and Lucy's all here
STOP   Your wire so comforting   STOP   My heart is broken
my mind fragmented but children keep me alive   STOP   A
later visit more helpful   STOP

Pete

August 21st, 1955

Dearest Pete:

   It's 11 o'clock here...5 o'clock in New York and I am sitting
quietly on the lanai, prayer book in hand, and with you in
spirit.

   Surely the church is filled to capacity and the flowers
overwhelming. I picture you and the children in the front
pew with Mr. and Mrs. Hopkinson and my prayers are for all
of you.

   Lucy is at peace now in a sunny room of Our Father's
mansion...just as Jesus has told us. I give thanks for her
days here on earth and for enriching our lives.

   I yearn to hold you, Ian, Em, and Lani, in a warm embrace
and share the tears that continue to fall.

   How may I help? I am so grateful that she sounded so
happy in her last letter. The enormity of this keeps creeping
into my mind awake and asleep and my compassion for you
is deep. In our shock and grief at this sudden loss, there is
disbelief and denial at first. That is when we must be

strong in our faith.

You know you can count on me for any help I might be able to give you or the children at any time. I know how Buzz would have left everything to be with his dear friend. Maybe he was even there to meet Lucy and Brett and lead the way into the light.

Lucy brought such joy into this world, and I count my blessings for our new-found friendship and all we shared.

Words seem so hollow, Pete, but I remember how you helped us through our grief just a few short years ago. Somehow the good Lord sustains us through the darkest hours and picks us up and carries us when we think we can bear no more.

Please give in to your sorrow, Pete, it does no good to keep it pent up. No regrets, dear Pete, you were a devoted and loving husband, and how Lucy loved you for your concerns and caring.

I'm sure that between the Hopkinsons and your family, the children are and will continue to be strengthened and sustained with love and attention and great affectionate solace. Their questions must be agonizing.

I keep looking out at the driveway and somehow I wish you were all coming here after the services. My heart aches for what each of you are going through and I only want to share this time with you so deeply.

Mama and Uncle Lot are writing you as I'm sure many, many others will be. Each letter will help, Pete, and maybe even bring a smile.

Don't feel pressed to write. I can wait patiently until you are ready and able to let the words flow on paper.

All my love,
Prudence

Kauai
August 25th, 1955

Dear Lani, Em, and Ian:

It's such a beautiful day today, and hope you're in Greenwich with Grandma and Grandpa and swimming whenever you can. Although I don't have a pool, I swim at the beach where I hope to take you some day.

I like to walk the whole bay looking for seashells, especially for the delicate angel-wing shells, and the tiny pink shells that make beautiful necklaces. It's always very exciting to find a big, blue-green glass ball. These balls are blown and formed in Japan by fishermen who use them for floaters on their fishing nets when they let them down way out at sea. Often these balls break away and float over the waves for a long, long time, over many miles, until they bob up in the surf off beaches in Hawaii and then on to shore. Of course, there are many small ones, but these big ones are what we all hope to find as prized treasures. When you come to Kauai, you can hope to find some, too. Ask Daddy if he ever found one.

Well, my dears, it's time for my supper so shall send this along with all my love. Hugs and kisses all around.

Your affectionate Aunt Prudence

Kauai
September 8th, 1955

Dear Ian, Lani, and Em:

Today I passed a schoolyard full of young children during recess, and suddenly realized you, Lani, must be back in school. What tales you will have to bring home to Ian, Em, and Daddy. I remember when I was in kindergarten. There was a jungle gym and a life-size playhouse and a garden. It was exciting to plant radish and carrot seeds in rows of neat little beds and wait for them to sprout. The radishes seemed to come up quickly and we couldn't wait to pull them up. Sometimes they were hardly ready to eat so we had to be more patient and wait until they were much bigger. Sometimes they were very, very hot.

Hopefully the books I sent have arrived and you are enjoying the stories. When I was your age, I loved the story about the pony growing up. My Daddy used to read it to me. I hope you like it, too.

Please give my love to Miss Mary and Daddy. I love you very much.

Love and kisses,
Aunt Prudence

New York
September 19, 1955

Dear Prudence:

It's hard to realize at times that Lucy has been gone a month already. I've tried to keep busy but it hasn't been easy. Hopefully the numbness may be beginning to wear off. My desk is stacked with letters which I want to answer, but somehow I can't bring myself to face this difficult and challenging task, so keep putting it off. I didn't realize just how many friends Lucy and I had and it's important to me that they know how much I appreciate their caring. However, tonight I feel I can only write you. For both of us, your friendship was something special and highly treasured...for which I am so thankful for now.

Please forgive my silence, Prudence. I have thought of you so often and just put off the misery of recounting the sad story to you. Tonight I can tell you. Perhaps after that I can face writing all our other friends.

We were all at Greenwich that Saturday morning enjoying a late breakfast and the twins kept agitating to get to the pool. Lucy seemed in no hurry to finish the food in front of her and, since I was finished, decided to appease their pestering and go on ahead. So I left her with the Hopkinsons.

About an hour later Miss Mary came running out to tell me Lucy wanted to see me...and from then, Prudence, I've lived and relived the nightmare of those next six hours.

Once we got Lucy into the hospital in New York, Dr. Harriman did all he could. As he explained it to me later, placenta abruption developed catastrophically and Lucy bled to death with our son. I keep asking myself if, in all that shock, anxiety, and rush, did I tell her how much I loved her and did she know I was anxiously pacing the corridors. I am still haunted by Dr. Harriman's face when he came out of the delivery room and walked toward me and the Hopkinsons. I couldn't relate this in the wire but now you know. We lost her to a fatal circumstance that rarely occurs.

Your keeping in touch was a great blessing, Prudence, and the children loved your letters which helped to distract them. Of the three, I think Ian is the most affected. He is quiet, and at times find him staring into space with thoughts miles away. We show them all the love we can, and I've had to be strong because of them.

The Hopkinsons were here with us for two weeks for which I shall ever be grateful. She brought two of her own staff with her and I was astounded at how, even in her own grief, she took over the running of the household so capably. Ever the diplomats, they quietly solved so many problems and helped me plan the funeral services. Miss Crowe was a godsend with the children.

Yes, the church was crowded and I can't describe to you the array of flowers – except to say there were many.

After the services I was thankful to have my family, as well as Lucy's, all here for comfort and company, and yet I felt like a survivor clinging to a log amidst a sea of rescuers who couldn't reach me. Ever thoughtful, they gave me space to mourn.

Only just a few days ago was I able to go back to the office, but found it hard to concentrate. Facing the sympathetic office staff was rather difficult too. Beginning with the boys in the garage and the elevator man, they were all so sincerely warm in their offerings of sympathy and love. I shall never take them for granted again.

Miss Mary has been a great support with the children, and I've made a point of coming home early to have dinner with the children in the dining room, reading a story at bed-time and tucking each in for the night. Lani still sleeps with the twins, but I think Grandma Hopkinson is planning a project with her to redecorate her room as an incentive for her to return to her own room. Being with them is a happy ending to a hard day of trying to make sense of these litigations which I somehow find so devoid of sanity.

Then the long nights begin. They are the hardest. No pillow talk to share our fears, hopes, and inner thoughts, our plans for the future and no warm body to love. Will I ever face the truth that Lucy is gone and no longer a part of my life? Life must go on, I know, and the children are now my life. I keep reminding myself that selfishly I'm forgetting the Hopkinsons' sense of loss, too, so make a point of sharing the children by spending weekends at Greenwich.

A part of me feels so exposed to the world and raw. I see Lucy all the time. The other day I thought I saw her in the midst of a crowd crossing 5th Ave. and found myself careening down the sidewalk. I try to keep my faith foremost, but must find the strength to turn a corner and re-enter the real world without her.

Please forgive my carrying on, Prudence, but there aren't many I can be honest with and it helps this heavy heart. I don't know what to say about coming East now. There is still so much I have to do in regards to Lucy's personal things and legal affairs. Nothing seems simple. I look in her closet and see a dress that reminds me of something we did together and I grieve for the past.

Please know how much your letters mean to me, Prudence, and though I have been silent and just now responding, please keep in touch...I appreciate that, and it helps.

> With fondest affection,
> Pete

Kauai
September 23rd, 1955

Dear Pete:

When I found your letter in the mail yesterday, I took it upstairs to my room to read quietly without interruptions, just as I did when you first wrote me after Buzz died. Your letters were always so comforting and helpful and even brought a smile. I know how hard it was for you to put pen to paper and tell me the tragic sequence of events and then to open up to your innermost feelings. After reading your letter my compassion for you is even deeper. I know, I've been there.

However, to lose a loved one so suddenly, especially the way Lucy went, must have been a traumatic time of utter disbelief and denial. With Mama and me, we had time to prepare for losing Buzz; and yet even though we thought we were ready, we certainly weren't. In either case, we go through the heartbreaking time when life seems to stop and nothing matters.

Pete, I share your feelings of utter loss and despair, but I assure you that somehow life does go on, even though we may seem so far removed from reality. Love is also a very powerful healing force, so let no negative thoughts or guilty feelings intrude in this experience. Having someone to love doubles our joys, and now you have the children to pour this love upon. In return, you are blessed with the love and solace they bring you. Also, the warmth of the love of family and friends that abounds will soon wear away some of the pain and help lift the veil of despair.

How thoughtful of you to share the children with their grandparents in Greenwich. They need lots of loving, too, especially Mrs. Hopkinson who was so close to Lucy. Hope by now Ian and Em are swimming in the deep end! I wrote the children, as I didn't want to intrude on your grief and yet wanted to keep in touch, too.

This morning I called Hal Faye, the ER doctor, to come to dinner so he could explain the facts of placenta abruption. Fortunately, he was free this evening and happy to accept. He was so understanding and told me in simple layman's language what had happened. He assured me that there was nothing Dr. Harriman might have done, especially since Lucy had been a very special patient.

As for my going East, this has been resolved by Kua and Hattie's decision to go to Sydney to be with her sister, who hasn't been in good health and has asked them to come for her 80th birthday in September. So the ranch will be my responsibility in his absence. Of course, you know Kua, he wanted to remain, but I insisted on his going and convinced him that everything would be fine...and it will be! Actually, I can't foresee any problems arising from the every day-to-day routine, but I do wish we could find a new manager so Kua would feel free to retire.

When the time is right and I feel the ranch story is finished – and it's far from that, I'm sorry to say – maybe I will plan to go East and see what can be done about publishing it. That's if your kind offer still stands to produce a publisher.

I'm looking at this happy photo of all of you taken at the christening, where Lucy is smiling down at Ian. I can understand his feeling of loss, as Lucy may have bonded more with her first son. I keep this framed photo right on a table near my desk.

So many happy memories of Lucy...finally meeting her and our immediate kinship, going through a distressing time with her that brought us closer together, her planning that Hawaiian feast to please you, her urging you to come to Mama's wedding, and her obvious devotion to you, Pete. Dwell on the happy memories and keep her memory alive by talking about her with the children, especially the funny stories and fun times you all shared.

Please hug them for me and know that nothing would please me more than to have them here on the ranch for a visit when the time is right. In the meantime, Pete, know that Lucy is smiling down at you and wants to see a big smile in response!

Fondly,
Prudence

New York
October 24, 1955

Dear Prudence:

Your comforting letter sits here but I don't want to bury it
under the stack of letters that are thankfully dwindling, as I
refer to it often. Everyone has been so kind and thoughtful,
and I hasten to tell you that you are so right...the love of old
friends and family is, indeed, heartwarming and helpful.
Some of my old pals have recounted the good times we
shared when we were courting our wives, times I had forgotten and yet came back so vividly. Lucy was such a good
sport and popular, too. How did I get so lucky?

My mother came and spent a few days with us, ostensibly
to do some early Christmas shopping in New York, but I
know that her real excuse was to see how I was doing and
check on the children. We crammed a lot into four days, and
I even took her to dinner one night. The children were delighted to have someone sincerely interested and eager to
listen to all their tales of woe and happiness. I can honestly
say she played no favorites, but several times I found Ian
looking at her intently and cuddling closer to her. She took
Em and Lani (she still wants us to call her that) shopping for
little girl things which lifted their spirits for days. So Ian and I
went to Schwartz to pick out a train set and met "the girls" for
lunch later. This proved to be such a happy time, and it did
us all so much good to be out doing something different
together.

Some time ago you mentioned something about women
bringing casseroles to newly widowed gents, and today I
found it all too true! A very attractive young divorcée who
Lucy and I knew just slightly as a neighbor, came to call on
Sunday evening with a casserole for my supper and a plate
of cookies for the children. Of course, the children danced

around her only too eager to sample their gift, but I must admit, Prudence, that I felt rather uneasy, awkward, and unnaturally inhospitable. I was afraid she was expecting to stay and share the casserole with me. Anyway, I did the best I could to seem appreciative, by thanking her profusely but professed to being in the middle of something very important and said goodbye. She is very attractive and I suspect lonely, too, but guess I'm just not ready for any female company at this point. Lucy is still very much a part of my life and guess there will never be anyone to take her place. Granted, the pain is less acute now and I can concentrate more at work, but things aren't the same by a long shot.

Lani's colorful artwork from school reminded me that Halloween is coming up soon, so I asked Miss Mary to buy a huge pumpkin which I shall endeavor to carve out with the children. Lucy was a kid herself when it came to Halloween and went all out to make special cookies for treats and create costumes, so now maybe I'll have to order some treats at the specialty shop on Fifth Avenue and take time off from work to take the children to Schwarz to find suitable outfits. The Hopkinsons have suggested a Halloween party for a few children and their parents early next Saturday, especially Lucy's good friend Annabelle, a widow with children the same ages. Then we'll take them trick-or-treating.

I'm not much into the party spirit, but must consider the children's pleasures and not be a selfish old stick-in-the-mud. If Halloween is any indication of the excitement surrounding this at school, what will Thanksgiving be like with all the pilgrims, Indians and turkeys? Heaven help us!

Friends have been so solicitous and included me in small gatherings, but when I finally decide to accept I find myself at a loss for words and keep looking for Lucy. I really don't feel a part of the group. Hopefully, this, too, will pass as I certainly don't want to be rude and seem unappreciative for being included.

I had a good letter from Asa Caldwell in which he extended a standing invitation to visit them at their place on the Big Island, and was even kind enough to specify Thanksgiving with the kids. His invitation reminded me of that famous Hawaiian hospitality so indigenous to the Islands. As tempting as it is, I can't see making the effort. I hadn't even considered making plans for Thanksgiving until his letter came. This will be a tough one, as Lucy always made so much over the holidays. Since it will be a school holiday and long weekend, maybe I'll take the children to my family in Philadelphia, but then I must consider the Hopkinsons, too, and their first Thanksgiving without Lucy. Well, time will tell.

Maybe I'm learning to take each day at a time. Had lunch the other day with an old Zete who is now a prominent M.D. in New York and I was rather surprised when he asked me how I was sleeping. When I admitted to tossing for hours missing Lucy, he prescribed some sleeping pills for me. He is quite the sympathetic guy. Since I realize it's important to get my sleep, I'm trying them with some success.

On re-reading this letter, Prudence, I realize it's been all about myself, so now I want to know what you've been doing. How are you coming on the story? My friend, the publisher, is still very interested in reading the manuscript when you are pau...say, how did I dredge up that word. See, you bring out the Hawaiian in me.

And what of the ranch? I hope things are going smoothly and that you'll find someone capable soon to fill Kua's shoes, not a simple chore!

I'll look forward to hearing from you with your news.

Fondly,
Pete

Kauai
November 6th, 1955

Dear Pete:

How joyous to find your letter on the upbeat side and your horizons broadening. However, I can readily understand your reluctance to join in friends' merriment. At least it was this way with me after Buzz died for quite some time, and I never quite understood why or how friends could continue merrily in their own pleasures when my heart was broken. Thankfully I had Mama to consider, and like you, didn't want to be a stick-in-the-mud. I think when we concentrate too much on our own grief that maybe we become selfish.

I wish I'd had some young to take trick-or-treating, but then I did have quite a few goblins come to call. I thought of you and the children at Greenwich trick-or-treating and hope all went well for you and no one suffered from over-indulgence. If you took any pictures of the children, I do wish you'd send me copies.

Had to laugh at the picture of the little lady down the street bringing you the fabled casserole! Have you returned her dish? That's the tricky part. Good luck!

Thankfully the ranch is going along well with no problems. I had a letter from a "dude" in Wyoming inquiring about the job but don't think he's suitable. If it was someone from the mainland, he should at least have had some exposure to Hawaii and its background to get along amiably with the local cowboys. No matter how competent he might be, these locals have their innate brand of working and living...a rare camaraderie that's truly Hawaiian, regardless of race.

Since the ranch is doing so well, I felt free to spend some time in Honolulu at the archives researching history of the ranch and Grandpa, which was all very rewarding. Also

Sara and Alika insisted I stay with them and we did have a wonderful visit. She has become quite involved in Kapiolani Hospital, the one where Buzz did most of his practicing. I wonder if it doesn't keep her closer to his memory in some small measure.

Mama and Uncle Lot have asked me to have Thanksgiving with them so am looking forward to that and hope to see the Caldwells. How kind of Asa to give you a carte blanche invitation. Maybe someday you'll be ready for that rare experience. Since Kua and Hattie will be back by then, I can spend the whole week up there. It's such a diversified island, with skiing at the top of Mauna Kea down to surfing in Kona, plus so many other natural attractions.

Please hug the children for me and lots of love to you, dear Pete. I'm anxious to hear a report on the casserole episode!

Wherever you'll be or whatever you'll be doing at Thanksgiving, know you have all my good wishes for a happy Thanksgiving. In spite of our losses, Pete, we have so much to be thankful for. God bless.

> Fondly,
> Prudence

New York
November 20, 1955

Dear Prudence:

So happy to hear all your news and rather envy your going to Hawaii for Thanksgiving. It was a hard call but the Hopkinsons couldn't have been more sympathetic and in agreement when I told them I'd decided to go to my family in Philadelphia for Thanksgiving. Then I thought, as long as we were facing important decisions, I would also think about Christmas. Christmas was such a special time for Lucy and I thought the children would be much happier here at home in familiar surroundings. So I've decided to stay home and make every effort to make the house festive and with lots of good cheer. At least I'll try, Prudence. I'm sure Miss Mary will enter into the spirit. I am grateful, too, that the Hopkinsons have agreed to have Christmas Eve dinner with us and stay at the Union Club that night to be with the children when we open presents Christmas morning. I'm not looking forward to this, Prudence, but I realize I must do this for the children's sake.

As the holidays approach, the formal invitations are beginning to come in the mail, but I think I've put my black tie away for quite some time. For the moment I am rather looking forward to going to Philadelphia and seeing some old friends. They are such low key "old shoe" that I know I'll feel very comfortable with them, I might even be able to take the children on a historical tour of the city. However, I don't think Ian is old enough to appreciate my old Zete house.

This brings ever so much love and hope that your visit to Hawaii will be beautiful, and if you see the Caldwells please give them my aloha. Yes, hopefully someday I will be there to see it all for myself.

Blessings at Thanksgiving, dear Prudence.

                    Fondly,
                    Pete

Kauai
December 2nd, 1955

Dear Pete:

What a great host Uncle Lot is, and the weather couldn't have been more cooperative. I had the same cottage right on the water's edge all to myself and loved falling asleep to the sound of the lapping waves over the black lava rocks.

Thanksgiving evening I thought of you so as we sat down to a groaning board and during the blessing prayed that you and the children were having a relaxing visit with your family and friends and enjoying the change of scenery. I'm sure your mother was delighted to have the grandchildren under her wings.

Uncle Lot's famous hospitality knows no bounds, and with Mama's graciousness they really do make quite a couple. Around sunset about twenty-four of us gathered on the lawn overlooking the ocean for cocktails then ambled over to the cookhouse for dinner. Mama had done a magnificent job of covering the tables with ti leaves and decorating them with colorful fruits and vegetables. She succeeded in converting the plain room into a bower of greens to make it so festive. Dining by candlelight was magical. Before we were finished dinner, the sound of music could be heard in the distance and soon the music boys appeared and sang the old favorites. There's something about Hawaiian music that is haunting yet romantic.

We spent a memorable day with Asa and Ginger, and I wish I had a picture of Mama jumping from the speedboat into waist-high waves on to the beach. She was laughing with delight when Asa caught her.

Their three children are delightful: the girl is Lani's age, there's a boy a few years older, and the other is about three. Ginger and I took them exploring along the beach for shells and what excitement when we found three small glass balls the high tide had deposited in the naupaka bushes. Please tell the children, as I've told them about these balls.

The Caldwells were delighted to hear news of you, Pete, and are hoping you'll come out sometime soon. Asa and Uncle Lot went fishing so we had their fresh catch grilled over the coals at lunch. Asa is devoted to his uncle and grateful for all he has learned from him through their fishing experiences.

Paulo took Mama and me down to that spectacular Kona coastline, dotted with inviting small bays and sandy beaches, and an awesome view up to the tops of Mauna Kea and Mauna Loa. After we arrived at the sleepy little town of Kona, we poked around the few curio shops and had a delicious lunch at the picturesque Kona Inn overlooking the little bay. I might venture to say that Kona is beginning to attract visitors and the charter fishing boats do a brisk business. Rosie Chong's, the local eatery, was packed with sun-burned malihini. It was hot, and we were thankful to get back to Puako for a cool swim in the pond. Uncle Lot had retrieved his lobster traps so we feasted royally that night.

For a change of climate and scenery, I accepted my old classmate's invitation to spend a few days at her family's ranch on the slopes of Hualalai. Her mother and father both come from a long line of old Hawaiian ranching families and they couldn't have been more hospitable. Their home reflects their love of Hawaii and is a treasure trove of Hawaiian stone artifacts found on the ranch, priceless heirlooms of calabashes of all sizes, finely woven mats, tapa, and a tall glass cabinet hung with feather lei, capes, and kahili. The house is furnished with priceless pieces of koa...tables, rockers, and graceful settees, and the hikiee are upholstered in fine lauhala matting. Mr. Holt gave me a super steed to ride around the ranch. It was a great interlude.

The happy couple is now planning a trip to Tahiti after spending Christmas at the ranch and New Year's in Honolulu. Mama is already beginning to think of Christmas Eve dinner following the children's service and toying with the idea of open house Christmas day. In the meantime I'll still have the ranch Christmas party and already shopping for that.

So now I'm back "in the saddle" and trying to concentrate on the story. It's good to have Kua back, and they both enjoyed Sydney and her sister's gala birthday party.

You're wise to be staying home for Christmas, Pete, even though it will be a difficult period of going through the pain of readjusting your life and facing the harsh reality of the first Christmas without a loved one. It can open up wounds we thought were healing, and the rawness hurts. But, Pete, Lucy will be with you in spirit and the children's excitement and anticipation will fill the void. I'm sure Miss Mary will see that the house is duly decorated, with the children's help, of course!

At Christmas I'm reminded of a quote from St. Matthew: "For where your treasure is, there your heart will be also."

All the heart-warming loving times with family and friends are treasures I can live and re-live again and again. What joy they bring.

I pray that all your tender memories are treasures you have stored in your heart, and that now they will transcend the past hurts.

Please try to enjoy the holidays and keep busy...Christmas shopping should do it! Hopefully you will feel up to joining old friends at a few small gatherings to lift the spirits. Will be anxious to know what you're planning.

So this brings my fondest love to you and the children

and for a merry, merry Christmas, Pete. Take care of yourself; you're particularly fragile at this time of year.

> Fondly,
> Prudence

New York
December 17, 1955

Dear Prudence:

Jingle bells are everywhere and the children are bursting with excitement. Miss Mary has the house decorated beautifully with all the familiar trimmings. Lucy used to spend hours decorating... even though she didn't feel all that great at this time last year. This year Lani's efforts from school have given the house a rather loving look.

The Hopkinsons are looking forward to being with us, and I've asked other family members here in the city to join us Christmas Eve in hopes of a rather festive evening. Fortunately, Mrs. Hopkinson has offered to work with a cateress for the dinner.

Yes, there have been a few small gatherings that I've been to and made every effort to enjoy until I started looking for Lucy to go home. Those sleeping pills my friend prescribed are really doing wonders, and I find my workload at the office is becoming far easier with a good night's sleep.

We had such a good visit at Thanksgiving with my family in Philadelphia and the children speak of their Nana so often, I've decided to spend the New Year's holiday with them and see my old pals again who were so solicitous. We drove down in November, but will go by train this time, and the children are excited over the prospect of a train ride.

The little "neighbor" down the street personally delivered

an invitation for cocktails, but thank goodness it was the same night as Lani's school pageant so I could be honest. However, she persisted that if I returned early to please join them. You know the answer. Thankfully, Mary had returned the casserole dish.

Happy that Uncle Lot and your mother will be with you for Christmas and know it will truly be a merry one. I can see you all now...cocktails on the lanai, gathering in that lovely big dining room around that handsome koa table, music boys bringing cheer and leading in singing Christmas carols...the true Christmas spirit! Please know I'll be thinking of you, Prudence, and at least trying to keep the Christmas spirit alive here.

This brings all good wishes for a very merry, merry Christmas and all the best for the coming New Year. Let's make it a good one!

As always,
Pete

P.S. In haste as shopping does keep me busy!

CHAPTER V

Philadelphia
January 1, 1956

Prudence Farnham
Kauai
Territory of Hawaii

Happy New Year   STOP   My grief overcome by childrens'
exuberant Christmas spirit   STOP   Enjoying my family and
old friends   STOP   Children enchanted with snowman   STOP
Your support has meant so much   STOP

Love,
Pete

Kauai
January 2nd, 1956

Dear Pete:

Happy New Year!!!

What a terrific way to start out the new year with your
cheery wire New Year's day! Keeping positive thoughts that
your good spirits will continue throughout the New Year. On
the surface it would seem as though you have hurdled the
first Christmas without Lucy, but I know differently.

Lei and Parker have been going to Honolulu every three
months for his check-ups, and the doctors are very
pleased with his progress. So they had a few of their old
friends in for their usual paina New Year's Eve, not as large
as the past ones, but full of aloha. Sara and Alika brought
great joy to all when they announced they would be parents
in June. Can't you see Lei with a moopuna! Nora and Hinano
are still the shy lovebirds.

Lei was kind enough to invite Bradley Carney, whom I'd
met at a dinner party and thought most attractive. He's
an artist and has rented a house in Poipu. I've been able to
toodle him around the island, pointing out scenic spots off
the beaten track and some familiar ones, too. I gather he is
financially independent so can devote himself full time to
his art, which I think is quite outstanding. His family lives in
Lake Forest where he grew up, but he showed no signs of
being hookano...you know, high hat...and entered right into
the spirit of the evening. Lei was pleased to see that he
seemed to be enjoying all the Hawaiian kaukau served at
midnight, and Parker even arranged it so that he got the
curly tail!

The story is progressing well and am including some fascinating tales of kahuna praying people to death as told to
Grandpa by the old-timers. Even today there are some who

still believe in the kahuna and the evil he can inflict on people with his praying over something belonging to the victim.

Still no luck in finding a manager and Kua has resigned himself to just staying on and trusting to fate or luck. The cowboys are delighted.

Am sure Mama and Uncle Lot are having a fabulous time in Tahiti with her old friend Mama Ettienne who, as a descendant of the last of the royal family, is revered and loved by the Tahitians. She will see to it that her guests relax and enjoy the experience of the true native way of life.

Not much news, really, but wanted to wish you all good things for the months to come in this New Year. Lots of love to you and children.

Fondly,
Prudence

New York
January 5th, 1956

Dear Aunt Prudence:

Thank you very much for the bracelet with my name on it. Daddy says it's a very extra special gift. I wear it all the time.

The twins love their presents, too. Em wore her muumuu all Christmas day. Ian slept in his cowboy shirt.

We had a good time at Nana's house. Daddy was such fun, too. He made a snowman for us in the front yard. He sure laughed a lot.

When are you coming to see us? I hope soon.

I love you.
Lani

New York
January 18, 1956

Dearest Prudence:

Things are pretty hectic here at the office after the holidays, but if I don't make the time to write you now, time has a way of slipping by.

You always seem to send just the right things to the children...it's a knack! Ian wore the shirt to bed Christmas night and all the next day. Em is a picture in her blue muumuu. Many thanks, Prudence. They'd write if they could but send you their thanks and lots of love.

We all had such a relaxing time in Philadelphia, and mother devoted her full attention to the children. As usual, my old pals were most cordial and sensitive to my needs.

The higher echelons are hinting about my going to Washington to do some work, but I'm protesting any such move. It's still too soon to leave the children, and no matter the cost, I shall remain firm in refusing to go.

Good to hear news of the Paoa family and the first grandchild. That Carney lad is a lucky guy to be able to stay in Kauai indefinitely, and you sound rather pleased for the company.

In haste but with lots of love, dear Prudence.

> Fondly,
> Pete

Kauai
February 4th, 1956

Dear Pete:

Have been in Honolulu doing more research on the ranch

and now have more than enough material, including old maps, dates, and pictures to keep me quite busy. It's nice to have Bradley for company in the evenings, although there's not much excitement on Kauai. He enjoys riding around the ranch in the late afternoon and cocktails on the lanai...and he loves to cook! So Matsu can have the night off. We've had some interesting meals! He has quite a sense of humor and has done some great sketches of the cowboys while drinking beer and talking story with them.

Unfortunately, one of my best sources of stories of Grandma, Lahilahi Waiwaiole, died last week at the ripe old age of 96. However, her memory was ever sharp whenever I visited her at her home on the plains of Mana. By the time all her generations of children and relatives from all the islands gathered, there was quite a crowd, from infants to the elderly. The ohana carried out her wishes, God bless them, to see that she had the most memorable funeral. Even in death she looked so regal, dressed in her black silk holoku with her yellow feather lei and her tortoise-shell comb in her white hair, lying in a silk-lined casket placed in the middle of the parlor and surrounded by flowers. Ladies from her society kept watch, intermittently waving kahili over the casket. Actually, Pete, you might compare this to an Irish wake.

One minute friends wept audibly over the coffin and then retired to the kitchen to wipe their tears, have a little inu of her rare okolehao and continue catching up with family. Only occasional muffled laughter or the cries of a baby disturbed the peace. Pau hana time the cowboys came to pay their respects by singing on the lanai until almost midnight. Family members took turns staying up with the body until the next morning when the hearse came to take her to the old church on the beach. After the services and burial in the adjoining graveyard, everyone returned to the house for a spread of food the likes of which you have never seen and lots of inu. I do believe this is the last of the old Hawaiian ways. Even the gods cooperated. That night around 1:00 a.m. there were and bright streaks of lightning to guide her way to heaven and booming claps of thunder announcing her safe arrival.

It all reminded me of the funerals for the old ranch hands when I was a child. Back then there were more of these wakes, and the eerie wailing and chanting for the dead by the mourners piercing the night were frightening. Buzz and the cowboys told me the kahuna were keeping the akua and ghosts away.

On a happier note, I've sent off some Valentines to the children and hope you all have a happy Valentine's Day. I'm sure Lani has been busy with the scissors and paste.

Lots of love, Pete, and hope things at the office aren't too demanding now.

As always,
Prudence

New York
March 1, 1956

Dearest Prudence:

We're all pretty excited here. The other night I was at a small dinner party and one of the guests was bemoaning the fact that he was stuck with the rental of a beach house on Kauai because now his children's activities conflicted with their plans to spend Easter vacation on Kauai. I don't know, Prudence, but it was as though I'd been struck by a bolt of lightning and woke up hearing myself saying, "I'll take the house over for you. Where is it exactly?"

I guess somewhere in the back of my mind I remembered your writing about the children's service and Easter egg hunt and picnic at the beach, and suddenly that's what I wanted for the children; to take them to Kauai for Easter and to see you.

Turns out the house is on the beach in Poipu, on the west side, and belongs to an old Island family who are traveling in Europe. I vaguely remember seeing the house at the end of the beach when Buzz and I went swimming and surfing in that beautiful bay. The realtor sent us pictures and we can have it for two weeks. Miss Mary is as excited as the children.

It may be stretching my good standing at the office to take off this way, but, Prudence, I truly feel this is a great opportunity for us all to have this time on our own and have an independent holiday. Please, I don't mean to exclude you because that's where the children's excitement really is...the ranch and your promise of beach picnics. I love their grandparents, but we'll be on our own this time.

So please put the dates down...April 3-17th. I'm renting the biggest car available, a station wagon. Hope you are as pleased as we are.

Asked an old friend about the Carneys, and he knew him at Harvard and through business on Wall Street. I gather your friend can well afford to paint on Kauai. Hope to meet him.

We leave on United from New York, spend the night in San Francisco, fly to Honolulu, change planes and arrive Lihue via Hawaiian Airlines at 11:30 a.m., April 3rd. See you then!

> Fondly,
> Pete

Kauai
March 11th, 1956

Dear Pete:

How exciting!!! Can't wait to see you all and will be at the plane to add to the arrival excitement! I can't think of anything better than having you with us Easter Sunday. Maybe the children will want to help us dye and decorate the eggs the day before. Oh what joy!

You'll love the house! I know it well, as the Taylors are old friends of the family. They built it as a beach house and over the years have made great improvements. The swimming in front of the house is the best on the island.

Kua and Hattie are looking forward to seeing you, too, as are Parker and Lei. They want to do something special for you and the children, too, but will leave plans until after you arrive. In any case, Kua is sending the cowboys down to the beach to cut kiawe wood for the fire in case there's a luau. He's also selecting particular horses for the children to ride safely. I must say, Pete, the cowboys are good with small ones, and very cautious, too. Their keiki have grown up in the saddle.

There's plenty of room at the ranch if you would like me to invite Asa and Ginger and their children for a few days. Might be a great reunion and fun for the children. I'll just extend the invitation anyway.

Mama and Uncle Lot are back after a dreamy time in Tahiti. He loved it. They had a house right on the water at Moorea, a little less civilized than Tahiti.With so many in help they were stumbling all over one another trying to please. Mama said the head chef excelled in a mixture of French and Tahitian cuisine that was most tasty and gave them some new ideas to try out, especially the dishes with coconut. Uncle Lot fished to his heart's content, and they even got over to Bora Bora. They want to return and spend some time there because it's so much like the old days in Hawaii. They really entered into the spirit of things. Mama wore a pareu and Uncle Lot the lavalava and brought back bolts of the colorful Tahitian print material and the native kapa, a lighter version of the Hawaiian quilt.

Bradley is really settling into the island ways and enjoying showing the island to a friend who is visiting him. Alan Somers is quite the dilettante and welcomed at a few parties we've been to.

Under separate cover am sending some coloring books of Hawaii for the plane rides.

Let me know what I can do. We'll at least have the cupboards stocked with food. It will be a glorious Easter with you and the children!

> Fondly,
> Prudence

Aboard United Airlines
April 17, 1956

Dearest Prudence:

Here we are flying above the clouds half way across the Pacific Ocean. After a rather tasty lunch, Miss Mary has the children settled down in hopes they'll doze off. They don't want to part with their lei and the aroma drifts across the aisle and has me thinking of those magical two weeks that went all too quickly. We all hated to leave, and it broke my heart to watch Ian clinging to you, not wanting to leave you. Poor little guy, he had such an exciting time and seemed to love just being with you, whether on the beach or just reading a book. I realize now how much he misses Lucy but doesn't want to let on.

To be back on the lanai just relaxing again was just what I needed, and even gathering everyone around the koa table for supper was so special...not to mention Matsu's taro muffins. You know they say that those who pray together stay together, and this was so true, not only at mealtime but especially on Easter Sunday when we all knelt to say the Lord's Prayer. I thought of Buzz as I watched the sunlight streaming through those stained glass windows.

Wasn't Lani funny when she tried to be a little above the excitement of the Easter egg hunt? As though it was only for the young! Finally she couldn't contain her excitement. She's quite a little lady for six going on seven and so protective of the twins, almost motherly.

The Kuakinis and the Paoas couldn't have been more hospitable, and I was happy to see Parker looking so well and active. I think the children were quite overwhelmed by the festivities of the luau, especially the men bringing the pig out of the imu. By any chance did you see how intrigued Em was watching the men handling those hot rocks? I guess I was enjoying the food so much they couldn't help but take to it, too, especially the haupia pudding.

It was good to see Alika and Sara and luckily have some time for a quiet visit with him. I wouldn't be surprised if somewhere down the road he doesn't move to one of the outside islands to practice, especially after the baby is born. He's a terrific gent and devoted to you, I can see.

After we get back, maybe this summer, I hope to find some place where Lani can continue her riding. I was so amazed all three took to it so quickly, especially Em, who loved the thrill of galloping with Kimo. But then you are so right! Those cowboys are at their best when with children. Those rides over the ranch lands with you were awesome. What beautiful country.

It was a treat to have the Caldwells and Uncle Lot and

your mother on the island at the same time. I can see where Asa and Uncle Lot have so much in common. That was so thoughtful of you to arrange it, Prudence. We had as much fun as the children, and Lani will be talking about the "sleep-over" at the ranch with the Caldwell children for quite some time.

The children were fascinated by Uncle Lot's tales of the ocean and Ian was bug-eyed, but Lani just clutched her Tutu's arm and looked up at her as if to say, 'is that true?"

All in all, Prudence, you made the visit totally successful. You look wonderful and what an ideal life you lead. I'm happy to see evidence of a fat manuscript and to know just where you are doing your writing. Very impressive. The children will sorely miss the beach and our picnics...I will, too, Prudence. Somehow I felt myself unwinding and relaxing for the first time in a long while and feel it's going to be rather difficult returning to the fast pace of New York.

I'm only sorry that the affair with Bradley has been a disappointment, but, Prudence, it is far better that you find these things out early on and can still remain friendly. I have known a few men who prefer their own sex and feel that what they do is their own business and I can still enjoy their friendship. Actually, they are good company and have a great sense of humor and can be most amusing. I rather liked Alan and found them both very intelligent and talented young men.

When we get home, I will have to give Miss Mary some time off, but am thankful that Miss Crowe will come in to care for the children. I'm sure she can cope with the twins. At least they're practically past the "terrible twos" but then they never were really that terrible!

Words can't express my gratitude and devotion to you, Prudence, but I think you know how much I appreciate all you did to make our visit so enjoyable. At least I have a lot of pictures to remind us all of the good times we shared.

My only regret is that we couldn't stay for the rodeo.
Maybe next year.

> Fondly,
> Pete

Kauai
May 4th, 1956

Dear Pete:

Things were so quiet around here for quite a few days after you left, and I just wandered around wondering what to
do with myself. I miss each and every one of you!!! When we
said goodbye, I could so easily have kept Ian here with me.
What a dear child he is, Pete. Yes, Em is the more spirited
and daring of the two and Ian may be considered the
shadow, but he has a very perceptive nature and for his
age, very alert to what is going on around him. The cowboys
still talk of Lani's riding ability and wish she could have
stayed a little longer to perfect a few points. She is a
beauty and has many of Lucy's characteristics. I love them
all! How fortunate you are to have Miss Mary.

Although Uncle Lot never had any children, he certainly
knows how to charm them. His stories about taking his dog
out surfing and the octopus sticking to his leg were really
about himself. Mama loved being called Tutu and can't wait
to have them visit Hawaii sometime. Uncle Lot would make
a fisherman out of Ian in no time. I can see it now.

Thanks for your good letter written homeward bound. I
kept thinking of you covering all those miles and was happy
to think of you safely back home. There was much more we
could have done, Pete, but there will be a next time, I hope.

Funny, isn't it, but when Alan appeared on the scene, I

didn't think anything of it. There had never been anything serious between Bradley and me, though I did enjoy his company very much and rather hoped it would blossom into romance. However, I'm not heartbroken. I am grateful for his tactful way of explaining Alan's presence. Of course, at boarding school we did have what we call "school-girl crushes" on girls, but I'd never been conscious of feelings between mature males. Sheltered life, maybe. However, as you say, they are good company and we have had some fun times. They had a high old time at the rodeo, Alan madly snapping pictures, and the cowboys seemed to accept them which is quite a test! If only Uncle Lot had been here when I first met Bradley, I don't think there would have been any doubt on my part. Uncle Lot tells it how it is!

I must admit it was rather difficult getting back to the discipline of writing, but I think I see the light at the end of tunnel. Grandma and Grandpa are both gone now and I'm going over it tying up loose ends. So maybe in a month or two, who knows, I can go East and see how your publisher feels about it. Any objections? Mama and Uncle Lot are planning a trip to Europe and I could go as far as New York with them which would be an experience. Anyway, time will tell and I'm concentrating very hard on the ending.

So I better get back to the work at hand, Pete, and send this off with lots of love to you and the children. Keep well and hope things aren't too hectic at the office.

> Devotedly,
> Prudence

New York
June 13, 1956

Dear Prudence:

The children never tire going over all the pictures of Kauai and remembering all the good times we shared. I know they miss you so hope you are nearing the end of the story so you will be coming to New York sooner. I wouldn't dare mention the possibility of your coming...their anticipation would be too overwhelming.

Miss Crowe took over the reins without a hitch and, of course, she spoiled the twins somewhat, but we were all happy which is the main thing. Miss Mary is back and reports a wonderful visit with her family in Ireland and brought back all sorts of Irish folk tales to tell the children. I even enjoyed a few stories, too. She is an enigma. She never speaks of her private life, but I gather she only has a very few friends here in the city besides her church, so considers us her family. She leaves Saturday mornings after breakfast and is back here after dinner on Sundays. I am so lucky to have such a levelheaded girl who knew Lucy.

We celebrated the twins' third birthday in Greenwich, as Mrs. Hopkinson had planned a little afternoon party for them and a few of their contemporaries. She even had a man bring a few ponies for them to ride. The youngsters were all quite excited, except Em who would have preferred a more spirited steed. They each had their own individually decorated birthday cake so blowing out the candles took a bit of time, but then they were anxious to get to their presents, too. Ian loves the cowboy shirt, Prudence, and Em is amassing quite a wardrobe of muumuu thanks to you. All in all it was a very special day and thought of you so much.

It's almost summer vacation for Lani and fortunately I've been able to sign her up for riding lessons in Greenwich on the weekends. The Hopkinsons welcome the opportunity to have them and are always considerate about not pressuring me to be there too. So unless I have an engagement in town, I usually go. For some reason or other if this proves to be too much for the Hopkinsons maybe we could change to the middle of the week when Miss Mary could be with them.

Sometimes I think it might be better to work something out during the week, as things are getting pretty hectic at the office and the pressure to go to Washington is mounting. On one hand I feel they were more than fair when I was going through a rough time, but then my place is still with the children, so I am dead set against the idea...come what may.

If things don't improve at the office, I foresee some serious problems and decisions, unfortunately. All these young lawyers whose careers were interrupted by the War are making up for the lost time and want to make the big-time sooner than later and don't mind stepping on or over a few toes. I don't like the scene.

Quite some time ago a friend who had gone through some difficult times asked me to join him and a group of men who meet informally once a month to discuss passages from the bible, prayer, and how their faith has sustained them. Since my life seemed to be at an impasse, I decided to join them and have been grateful ever since. I think one of the hardest things I've ever had to do after losing Lucy was to face the fact she was gone, pick up the pieces, and carry on. It must have been the hand of God that led me to this group.

I have been going every month now for at least six months, and the support and encouragement this group provides has proven invaluable. I might even compare it to AA. Several times a call to one of the members has been so helpful. I'm surprised how many passages from the bible became so much clearer. I know now more than ever that God is always there...a source of comfort that gives me the courage and hope to face the future with peace of mind. Faith and positive thinking are powerful assets that can bring great inner peace.

The Kauai visit was just what I needed, Prudence, and as I predicted, don't much like facing the fast pace of the city after such a relaxed and peaceful time on that beautiful island. We all want to come back! In the meantime please let me know when you'll be coming to New York. What a time we'll have if your mother and Uncle Lot are here, too.

Lots of love as always,
Pete

Kauai
June 30th, 1956

Dear Pete:

Thrilled to hear that Lani will be continuing her riding lessons. I do hope things work out for the best for everyone, but distressed over the situation at the office. Being a single parent can't be easy, and being responsible for three active children is a great challenge that you have been able to handle very well, Pete. I've never heard of a men's liturgical group but it seems to be helping you immeasurably. I do know that the prayer group at our little church has done miracles for some people, and yet they are reluctant to discuss this great power that prayer can evoke.

Bradley had a successful showing of his works at a small local gallery, that really benefited by the opening reception, and Alan hopes to have a showing of his black and white photos some day, too. People have really taken to Bradley and Alan, and they've become quite the popular "extra men" at parties. Bradley is always the gentleman, and I do enjoy their company.

Sara had a little boy. Parker and Lei couldn't wait to get over to Honolulu to see their first moopuna. I feel so honored. They want me to be his godmother and the christening will be at the cathedral where they were married on July 8th. Mama would like to go, too, so think I'll stay with them at the Halekulani. The Carringtons are having a small celebration after the baptism.

Yes, I think I can truly say I'm finally coming to the end of the story. Mama says they are leaving August 18th for San Francisco, spending a few days, then flying to New York, Sept. 1st. So if those dates are agreeable with you I'll be on the plane with them. Uncle Lot likes to stay at the Carlyle, so guess that's where we'll be unless they can't give him a suite. Then we'll go to the Waldorf. He certainly has his definite preferences.

Just thinking about being in New York and seeing you all again is sheer happiness. Of course, I can't help but think of our last visit to New York and what Lucy and I went through, but we mustn't let this overshadow the visit, Pete.

If you could arrange a date with your publisher friend, I would so appreciate it and look forward to the propitious day. I have given the manuscript to an English teacher at the local high school to read and make any needed corrections. Then I shall give it to someone to type professionally and have at least three copies made. I hesitate to let you read it until after we hear from the publisher and then maybe I'll be brave enough to let you look at it. It's far from a masterpiece but I think it covers a good slice of life in Hawaii from the early 1800s to the 1950s.

There's a round-up tomorrow and I spent the day checking the horses' hooves so best get ready for a long day and say goodnight.

Fondly,
Prudence

New York
July 15, 1956

Dear Prudence:

Have September 1st circled in red on calendars at home and the office. Count on an enthusiastic welcoming committee consisting of four. I haven't told the children the good news yet but will do so as the time draws nearer. Dave Putnam, the publisher, is looking forward to seeing you on September 3rd at 10 a.m. at his office at Bell Books. You'll like him, he's about my age, and for goodness sakes, don't be nervous as there's "nothing to fear but fear itself". I just feel certain that you have a winner.

How I look forward to having you in New York, Prudence, but am not planning anything until you get here, especially with your being with Uncle Lot and your mother. I'm sure he has numerous New York buddies who are champing at the bit to see him and his bride and reciprocate their hospitality. However, I do have several mental plans I hope to execute when time allows. The Hopkinsons are hoping you will be able to go to Greenwich for lunch one day, preferably when the children can be there, too. But you name the day.

I have to admit one thing...Mother is so anxious to meet this famous "Aunt Prudence" that she'll be coming over to spend one night so we can all have dinner. Hopefully, Dad will join her, but he's not all that keen on being away from his dogs and routine. However, he knows he's invited.

Lani is loving her riding lessons and adapting well. Midweek has proven the better choice for the duration of the lessons and it gives me more time at the office without the pressure of being home for the children. Usually have dinner at the club so don't want for company.

Was at a small gathering for cocktails last week and the "neighbor down the street" was there also. She is attractive but so obvious in her hopes for a bit of companionship. Frankly, not my type.

Looking at the calendar, I see you'll be leaving Kauai soon. Have a great time in San Francisco and save lots of energy and time for me in New York. Until we meet...

Love,
Pete

Kauai
August 6th, 1956

Dearest Pete:

Can't wait to see the committee of four...at the Waldorf! I'm afraid you'll have me on your hands more than you anticipated, as Mama and I have discussed our stay in New York and we both realize that their time will be taken up with all Uncle Lot's friends. I'm sure they're all very interesting, but truthfully I'd rather be with you and the children. So I'd love to have lunch at Greenwich and look forward to meeting your mother. I know that Mama wants to meet her, too, after her warm letters after Buzz died, and hopes to arrange a dinner.

Mama and Uncle Lot sail on the Queen Mary Sept. 15th and I've booked passage on United for a flight to San Francisco the next day at 1 p.m.. Two weeks is a long time, Pete, so please don't feel responsible for entertaining me! I hope that I will be spending a lot of time with your Putnam friend over the book. I'll try to be casual, as though handing over a manuscript was routine...however, Pete, I am nervous!!

Am rather looking forward to seeing some old friends in the Bay Area and will be on my own there, too. We'll be headquartered at the Huntington Hotel, where Uncle Lot keeps an apartment, but I'll have my own room. It's a bit off the shopping path, so will either be hiking the hills or supporting the taxi industry.

Kimo Carrington Paoa behaved like a little angel at his christening in Honolulu. He's a handsome baby, large brown eyes and dark hair like his father, and quite alert during the ceremony, too. Parker was about to burst his buttons with pride and dear Lei couldn't keep back the tears of joy. The Carringtons had us all to their home for dinner after the five o'clock service, and I had a chance to have a lovely visit with the bishop, who performed the service. The gods are really smiling on Sara and Alika.

Pete, it will be so good to see you again and am looking forward to being with the children. I hope to spend a lot of time with the twins during the day, going to the park and maybe even have some picnics.

The typist returned three clean copies of the manuscript and I have them all ready to go with me. Oh, Pete, wouldn't it be exciting if it were accepted and published! A dream come true, and Grandpa's life story preserved.

Must tend to some ranch business with Kua and leave with a clear conscience. So pau for now and it won't be too long now!

Fondly,
Prudence

P.S. Please know that I will be thinking of you with special prayers on the 19th. The first anniversary is always the hardest, I know, but time, faith in the future, and lots of love have great healing powers. God bless.

Kauai
September 19th, 1956

Pete, Dear:

Oh, how I hated to leave New York and the welcoming committee! All the way home I kept re-living the memorable times we shared. Lunch at Greenwich with the Hopkinsons couldn't have been nicer, and how she adores the children. I remember Lucy used to refer to her father as "Ole Pops," and somehow the name just fits him. I wanted to wrap up your mother and bring her home with me. What a warm, darling person she is, Pete, and we had the best time with the children. Lunch with them and Mama and Uncle Lot at the Waldorf was a bonus and so glad you could join us. Your mother and Uncle Lot seemed to hit it off beautifully, and of course, the children enjoyed seeing him again, too. I'm only sorry your father didn't come to New York. That was a super day.

How grateful I am for the time spent with Dave Putnam. I liked him immediately. Nothing like starting at the top, when he could just as well have turned me over to an assistant. He was so easy to work with, and I shall now concentrate on producing more pictures and identifications. Dave made some excellent points on the editing and changes and, of course, it does sharpen the story immensely. I just can't believe it, Pete...my story is going to be published!!! And it's all because of you!

Whether we were having dinner with the children at home or alone, Pete, those times were always so rewarding and special. The house radiates the charm and warmth Lucy created and the children are so happy there. You were so relaxed, and we never seemed to lack for conversation. Yet it felt comfortable just enjoying being together quietly.

Dear little Ian. He's grown so since I saw him in April. I

surmise that Em is the apple of Mrs. Hopkinson's eye, although she tries not to show any favoritism. Lani will never lack for friends. She has a fantastic personality for one so young and attracts people like a magnet.

Oh, Pete, why do we all have to live so far apart! I miss you so. It's going to be hard settling back down to life on Kauai after all the glamour of the trip and Mama and Uncle Lot way off in Europe. However, I shall survive. This, too, will pass.

Called Bradley to say I was back and they're coming for dinner next week and bringing a houseguest, an elderly lady from New York. This will be interesting.

The only unpleasant note of the trip was realizing that things aren't going well for you at the office. I found your senior officer, Jim Grant, quite charming socially, but am sure he can be a bear in business. I knew a man like that in Honolulu...perfect gentleman, but in the office, beware. He drove a hard bargain with the unions and could match them drink for drink during negotiations.

Was able to write my thank-you notes on the plane and found writing your mother the easiest. Wouldn't it be great if she could come out to visit the Islands?

Actually, without the story to take up my time, I feel rather lost and guess I'll just get back to riding again. Maybe I'll get involved in some volunteer work at the museum. I'll see.

Dear Pete, thanks for just being you and clucking over me in the big city. I loved it!

Fondly,
Prudence

New York
September 29, 1956

Dearest Prudence:

Your letter succeeded in stirring up all the fond memories of our time together in New York, and the children keep asking when you're coming back. Yes, when will that be! Maybe you'll have to come East for the launching of your book.

I knew you'd like Dave. I saw him at lunch the other day and he reported the book is right on schedule and seemed quite pleased the way things are going. You did it all yourself, Prudence, and I'm proud of you!

Yes, you were so right about Jim Bradley. The situation at the office was coming to the point where I either had to cut bait or sink, so I made a trip down to Philadelphia to talk things over with my father who I've always turned to in time of indecision. He listened attentively, mulled it all over quietly, looked me in the eyes and said, "My advice to you, Pete, would be to resign now while no one has been hurt and there is no obvious dissent." I knew it was the thing to do but wanted to hear it from him.

That was two weeks ago, and I kept pondering over the best approach to take. It was a tough call, but I had to do it, Prudence. Three days ago I handed in my letter of resignation as of October 31st. Later, Jim came into my office visibly upset and asked me the meaning of the letter. He kept things pretty much under control, but, by the same token, was trying to get me to give him reasons and hoping to change my mind. As a gentleman I really couldn't put the blame on anyone so explained it was solely for personal and family reasons. Jim knows the children are so much a part of my life now and without coming right out and hiding behind that excuse, I made myself quite clear that there was no turning back or changing my mind. This was it.

He took me to lunch, we had a drink...you know I don't drink at lunch...and I walked back to the office as though on air, completely relieved of a heavy burden, both physical and mental. Later I started cleaning out my files and amazed at what I discovered. I'm saving the little notes Lani has written me and a few drawings of the twins, naturally, but so much went in to the trash basket.

Of course, my secretary had typed the letter of resignation so I hurdled that one rather easily, and am positive she shall soon begin an excellent job. With no plans in mind, I'm wondering whether I'll be needing her in the near future.

So there you have it, Prudence. I'll be pau at the office in a month. I still can't believe it. When I called my Dad, he was delighted. He said I'd never regret the move and would never lack for work.

Wish you were here to go out and let off some steam tonight!

I've decided not to say anything to the children until around the end of October and then we can maybe go to Philadelphia for a long weekend with my family.

Met with Lucy's executor the other day, and things are pretty much wound up. She was very generous in her bequests to her favorite charities and very specific in designating certain pieces of jewelry to family and friends and artwork that were to go to siblings, close friends, and Miss Crowe. Hope you'll enjoy wearing her jade pin, a favorite of hers.

One of the hardest things I've had to do was go through Lucy's closets and dressers with her mother. I knew it had to be done, but I kept putting it off until it began weighing heavily on my conscience. Just looking at the perfume bottles on her dressing table brought back too many memories. So one Saturday morning after we returned from Kauai, Mrs. Hopkinson came in with her faithful housekeeper and we began the sad process. By five o'clock we had bagged and tagged everything and both felt that Lucy would have wanted us to give her clothes to deserving charities with profitable thrift shops. It wasn't easy, Prudence, and several times Mrs. Hopkinson and I were suddenly overwhelmed...but why go on when you know how it was going through Buzz's things.

Please excuse the ramblings, but you're one of my best listeners. I feel like the proverbial new man. Now I am beginning to see the trees. Otherwise, not much news really, the children are fine, and we all think of you often.

Take care and that's a good idea to find some volunteer work to keep you out of mischief.

Fondly,
Pete

Kauai
October 16th, 1956

Dearest Pete:

Although I knew things at the office weren't going well, news of your resignation came as quite a surprise today. I'm sorry for all the agony and tribulations you've been through, Pete, but what a blessed relief this decision must be. You have shown great strength of character by resigning without implicating anyone or disrupting harmony in the office. I'm sure it wasn't easy and required great patience and tact. You've done a brave thing and I just know that something much better will arise from the ashes. Your father is so right. Congratulations!!!

Hopefully, this last month at the office will go smoothly and your Philadelphia visit will bring great joy and satisfaction. A visit there always seems to pep you up and the children love being with their Nana. Please send her my aloha.

Sara and Alika were here with the baby for the weekend, and Parker and Lei insisted that they were perfectly capable of managing Kimo and sent Sara and Alika off to spend two days at the ranch beach house. Alika really needed the respite and Kimo was an angel. According to Sara, he's been working overtime at the hospital and not getting home until around eight o'clock. I keep thinking of what you said long ago, that you wouldn't be surprised if he practiced on a neighbor island...and I wonder if he isn't thinking along these lines now. We sure could use a good O.B. man here.

When Bradley and Alan heard I was riding in the afternoons, they asked if they could join me. Thank goodness they are both excellent horsemen because I took them through some pretty wild country to get some exclusive shots. I am forever grateful to Grandpa's foresight in establishing the ranch.

Your mention of a thrift shop has set my mind racing and I want to discuss it with Nora. A thrift shop to benefit the local hospital would be a terrific moneymaker and an opportunity for struggling families to find needed clothing and household goods at bargain prices. Children grow so fast that clothing is a big item in the budget. First, I'd have to start looking around for an empty house in a convenient location, large enough to display things properly and yet have ample storage space. This will be a great project. I have the time, and am sure people will be most generous with their support and donations of clothing and household items. Wish me luck, Pete.

So, dear Pete, thank you for sharing your news and am so happy for you. You've taken a giant step, so please take your time planning for the future. Hope the children are thriving and please give them each a big hug for me.

Fondly,
Prudence

New York
November 8, 1956

Prudence, dear:

My fist week of leisure has been spent concentrating on my future plans and proposals that I want to share with you. In one of my first letters to you after Buzz died I remember asking if I could be your big brother. Then I think in another I said something to the effect that with Buzz gone my reason for settling in the Islands was gone, so could we please keep my ties to the Islands alive through our correspondence. Can't remember which letter it was that I said Buzz and I were so close that I loved the things he loved.

Well, you and I have been writing back and forth for four years now, and you have kept those ties to the Islands alive so I've always had a close rapport with you. We have shared so much, especially after your trip East and being with Lucy at a crucial time. After Lucy died, I finally turned to you first to pour out my heart. Between my trip to Kauai with the children when we did, indeed, share the Easter service with the balloons rising significantly to heaven, and your trip East, I felt suppressed feelings emerging...happiness and contentment I hadn't felt for a long time. Now I realize it was love for you.

What I'm proposing now, dear Prudence, is that instead of being your big brother, I want to be your husband. I love you very much and know for certain that our marriage would be a happy one for me and the children, as I would hope, for you. I wouldn't ask you to live in the East but would ask you to please consider me as the new ranch manager. With my legal background and my early years in the Islands I might just qualify.

Dear Prudence, I have been doing a lot of thinking about my future, and it seems wherever I turn you are there. You have become so much a part of my life, and the visit to Kauai really opened my eyes to all your fine qualities, the quality of life there, and how much we four need someone like you in our lives.

As you know, I have always loved the Islands and a part of my heart has always been there – at least since I was fifteen. Now I'm forty years old and want to reclaim my heart.

This last visit to Philadelphia was wonderful, and I shared my thoughts with my father and mother and they couldn't be happier at the idea, Prudence. I am sure that when I tell the Hopkinsons after hearing from you, they, too, shall be pleased. Of course, Lucy will always remain a blessed memory for me, but, Prudence, I feel in my heart, too, that Lucy would want this marriage. She was so fond of you and knew how much the children adored you.

I can't wait to hold you in my arms and whisper I love you. My love is true and strong, dear Prudence, and I'm sending it in this letter and anxiously awaiting your reaction. I do hope it doesn't come as a complete surprise because you must have felt some sparks of emotion when we were together on Kauai and here. I feel as though I've awakened from a long sleep and found you by my side. I yearn for an early wedding. Will you please be my bride?

Anxious but devoted,
Pete

Territory of Hawaii
13 November 1956

Peter Thorne
72nd St.
New York, N.Y.

Your happiness is my happiness   STOP   Can't wait to tell
you I love you   STOP   Too excited to write   STOP   Letter
shredded from rereading   STOP   Anticipating loving
husband and fantastic ranch manager   STOP   Does small
December wedding on lanai sound plausible   STOP   I'm
anxious too dear Pete   STOP   Please tell children I love
them   STOP

All my love
Prudence

Chapter VI

Kauai
June 10, 2002

Gay, dear,

The whole family was here for a glorious Easter, and
how I wish you could have been here with us. However,
the journey from Germany is an ordeal anyway and the
doctor was so right to forbid you to travel in your 7th
month. I certainly wouldn't want anything amiss for my
first moopuna.

The enclosed is what I have written to put with the letters back in the safe. If you can add anything, or have any
suggestions, please call me.

I love you very much. Take care of yourself and hope
Fritz isn't too busy at the embassy.

Fondly,
Mom

MOM AND DAD'S LIFE

We found Mom and Dad's correspondence quite by chance, as no one had ever told us of the secret compartment in the monstrous koa armoire with glass doors that had stood at one end of the dining room for four generations. It held rare Hawaiian artifacts found on the ranch, feather work, calabashes, finely woven makaloa mats from Niihau, and miscellaneous trophies. I must have knocked against one of the heavy carved pineapples protruding from the frame of the cabinet, which triggered a drawer to slowly slide out from under the bottom drawer.

Now that all the family has read the letters, Kulia has urged me to fill in the years up to the present so we can put the story and letters together in the safe for future generations.

I have read and re-read the letters, and each time gain more insight into their lives and how their friendship and compassion for one another led to romance. They are both gone now. Dad was diagnosed with melanoma and died in 1991 at the age of 76. Two years later, after Mom's horse galloped back to the barn, the cowboys went out to search for her and found her lifeless body lying against the lava rock wall bordering the entrance to the family graveyard. We took comfort in believing that she was on her way to join Dad. She had been in the habit of riding up to the mountains to pick maile and weave a lei to take to his grave. They had been married thirty-five years. Thirty-five happy and productive years.

After Walter was born in 1958 and Kulia in 1960, Mom never ever showed any favoritism, and we were one family. When Mom's book about the ranch went out of print, it became a collector's item and since being republished, has become a Hawaiian classic on ranch life in the Islands. She also wrote fascinating children's books based on old Hawaiian folk tales that captivated us kids when she tried out scripts on us. We must have been capable critics, as they were all bestsellers.

The cowboys took to Dad immediately. They liked the way he entered into the spirit of ranch life, eager to learn from them and listen to their ideas. Any changes he made were well thought out, had everyone's approval, and done gradually. He knew each family member by name, which meant a lot to these gentle people, and he always had a good word for everyone.

How well I remember going out on my first cattle drive with Dad and his friends, the cowboys. The moon was still high up in the sky at 2 a.m. when we started rounding up the cattle to drive them down the mountainside. It was the first of many thrilling cattle drives, and it was so special being with Dad.

We were such a happy family, very close, and always tied to the ranch. Losing Dad was so sad. We think it was his constant exposure to the strong rays of the Hawaiian sun that caused the melanoma. I am the first to admit that we all fell apart after Mom died, but found great solace in being together at the ranch that held so many precious memories for each of us.

We owe our Christian life style to Mom and Dad, who were the best examples of the true values in life, and we grew up in the church and lived the Ten Commandments. We shall always consider little St. John's our home church, where Walter and Kulia were christened and all confirmed, although I was the only one to be married there. Our family still attends the children's Christmas Eve service.

None of us older kids really remember much about living in the East. Mom had always been the only mother we really knew. Dad always came first, but she devoted her life to us, gave us all her attention and love even after we left home for school, college, and eventually marriage. I, for one, shall always be grateful to her for nurturing my love of nature and horses. We had so many adventurous rides on the ranch, and I often retrace our paths and think of her so fondly.

I must have been eight when Mom and Dad were married and remember very little of that day on the lanai except all the excitement and romance a wedding holds for a young girl. So I never tired of hearing different versions of the wedding. I do remember Dad kneeling down to embrace me and the twins and telling us that Aunt Prudence would be our Mom just before they were married, and having our grandparents all there.

Our visits to Hawaii always awaken many happy memories. My fondest memory is of Grandpa Lot, who had a great influence on the family's understanding of our Hawaiian heritage and the old Hawaiian ways of life. I'll always remember his telling us that we couldn't be keiki o ka aina unless we knew the difference in sound between the waving bamboo and rain. Eventually we had to put up a bunk house for all the kids on his place, and each year we make every effort to gather there as a family to celebrate Thanksgiving and give thanks for Tutu and Grandpa Lot. They certainly enriched our lives.

Because I was the oldest and never lost my love for the ranch after Mom helped me up into the saddle of the first horse I ever rode, the siblings agreed that my husband and I should take over the reins of the ranch. Sam and I have been married for twenty-eight years now and have three children who have had the wonderful experience of growing up on a ranch. Like Dad, Sam was a lawyer in Honolulu before we decided to take over the management of the ranch, and he has never regretted it.

Growing up surrounded by family treasures and antiques in his Grandparents' and Tutu's homes, Ian was aware of and appreciated fine things. He apprenticed at Sotheby's in New York then went to London where he now has his own antique shop. He welcomes people from Hawaii, so is always on the alert for Hawaiiana in England and on the Continent. He's still a bachelor.

Em went from blocks to becoming one of the top architects in Hawaii. She concentrates on Hawaiian-style houses that take advantage of the tradewinds, and she favors large lanai over family rooms. Her husband, Kauru Suzuki, is a leading dentist in Honolulu and they have two bright children.

Walter pursued medicine and married a charming, part-Hawaiian girl. They moved from Honolulu to Molokai where he is a beloved family doctor. They named their daughter Prudence, and their son, Pete.

Kulia, always a lover of Hawaiiana, works as a volunteer at the Bishop Museum while raising a family of five. She married Kaimi Holt, one of the heirs of the largest estates in the Islands. He keeps active in real estate. They are both pleased that all the children opted to go to Kamehameha School, founded by Princess Pauahi, over the missionary-founded Punahou School.

Of all our beloved ranch family members, we were all grief stricken and weighed down with so many memories when Kua died at the age of 95. A bit of our hearts went with him. He taught us all the old Hawaiian songs and how to play the ukulele and guitar. Fortunately, he was endowed with a lot of patience. He was his old dear self until the morning Hattie found him sleeping peacefully. Hattie is in her late 80s now and will never leave Kauai. Hinano and Nora finally persuaded her to come and live in a cottage on the grounds of their lovely home.

Parker died in his late eighties, and Alika was a pillar of strength for Lei and finally convinced her to come and live in a retirement home in Honolulu to be near them. Actually, she loves babysitting their three children. Alika never left Honolulu and now has his own clinic, staffed with outstanding specialists.

Bradley Carney is an admired artist in the Islands. Mom had always been a great admirer of his work and kept up her friendship with him and Alan. I can't remember their ever missing Thanksgiving or Christmas dinner with us and I grew to appreciate their sense of humor and philosophy on life. After Mom died, Bradley was always ready to share his memories of meeting Mom when he first came to Kauai, and admits his success is largely due to her encouragement.

Bradley and Alan became pets of the widow Fanny Harrison and spent much time at her estate on one of the finest secluded bays on the island. Many of Brad's best works were done there. None of us were surprised when Fanny left the property to them. It suits their style of living and entertaining interesting people from around the world. Invitations to their annual costume ball are coveted and well attended. Even Ian came one year.

Mom always considered Hal Faye an old friend on whom she could rely for a second opinion. He was there when Dad was so sick. Hal never left Kauai after he became the head of the emergency unit. Mom was so pleased when he married an attractive nurse he had known for quite a while.

Yesterday was Mom's birthday. She would have been 80, much too young to no longer be with us. That afternoon I strung some lei and rode up to the family cemetery. After placing lei on the headstones of Great Grandpa and Great Grandma, Tutu, Uncle Buzz, Fusako, and Mom and Dad, I sat under the lehua tree bursting with red blossoms, and found myself going back in time. Except for Mom's book about Great Grandpa, I never knew him or Great Grandma but always felt I did from hearing Mom's stories. I never knew Uncle Buzz either, but people still speak of him endearingly. Tutu, I remember very well for all the kindness and love she gave us kids. I still miss her. Dad, bless him, couldn't have been a better father. He quietly taught us so much. Dear Fusako lived with our family and gave us so much love. She sometimes even spoiled us. She would be so gratified to see what happiness she has brought to so many.

Then my thoughts turned to Mom and all the good she had done in the community. I still miss her, especially when I want to run back to her and tell her a funny incident.

She was able to buy 10 acres of beachfront property adjoining the ranch beach house with the idea of creating a summer camp for children suffering from cancer in remission. Named for her grandfather, "Kauka's Camp" has proven to be an answer to prayers and well supported by the community. When Hal Faye retired, it didn't take much urging to have him become the camp's doctor. Today, the board of trustees include many influential kamaaina and those who are strong supporters of the fight against cancer.

The thrift shop mom began many years ago has doubled in size and continues to keep up her strict standards of clean, used clothes in good condition, working appliances, fresh baby needs, books, and miscellaneous tempting merchandise. The shop never lacks for contributions or volunteers. Every year the proceeds are distributed among the several local charitable organizations.

How these good people would mourn in disbelief the closing down of sugar plantations in the Islands with the exception of two profitable companies. Those plantations were communities unto themselves and sugar was king. Today the Democratic Party and labor unions have strong leaders on Kauai.

We can only hope that each of them would be pleased to see the ranch still operational and following family traditions, two of which we faithfully observe being the Christmas party for the ranch families and the rodeo celebrating Prince Kuhio's birthday. Christmas brings the ranch together as one big family with lots of aloha, and the cowboys look forward to the yearly competition.

Lost in my warm thoughts of these people, I was reluctant to leave. As I rode back down through pastures, I thought of the future. It is my sincere hope that the future generations will honor their ancestors' wishes and make it a point to watch over the ranch to the best of their ability and see that the family cemetery is kept up with the utmost care. I would like to think that these descendents will always return to pay homage to the family that founded a strong dynasty by taking the time to come back and place lei on the headstones of their beloved ancestors.

Mounting the lanai steps, a wave of nostalgia overcame me and I thought, "If only this lanai could talk."

Lani Grant
May 19th, 2002
Kauai, Hawaii

GLOSSARY

Aikane	friend
Akua	ghost
Alii	chief, royalty
Aloha	love, hello, goodbye
Aumakua	family guardian or god
Calabash cousin	long-time friend, almost part of the family
Ehu	red, reddish
Groaning board	a table laden with food
Halau	long house
Hana	work, job
Hanai	foster, adopted
Haole	white person
Hapa	half
Hapai	pregnant
Haupia	coconut pudding
Heiau	sacred native place of worship
Hikiee	large, comfortable couch or bed
Hila Hila	shame
Holoku	formal Hawaiian dress with train
Hookano	snobbish, haughty
Hoolaulea	celebration
Hula	native Hawaiian dance

Huna	Hawaiian healing
Ilima	fragile yellow blossom
Imu	Hawaiian underground oven
Inu	drink
Kahili	feather standard
Kahuna	Hawaiian priest
Kamaaina	native Hawaiian
Kanaka	slang term for a Hawaiian
Kapa	Hawaiian quilt
Kaukau	food
Keiki	child
Keiki o ka aina	child of the land
Kiawe	algaroba tree
Kimono	Japanese robe
Kolohe	naughty
Kukui	nut used for light, relish
Kuleana	property
Lanai	outdoor living room
Land shells	native snails now almost extinct
Lauhala	native pandus used for mats
Laukahi	green plant used for healing
Laulau	native bundle of luau leaves and meat wrapped in ti leaves and steamed
Lawalu	bake in ti leaves
Lavalava	cloth worn like a kilt or skirt
Lehua	flower of the ohia tree
Lei	garland
Lomi	massage

Mah-Jongg	game of Chinese origin
Mahalo	thank you
Maile	fragrant green leaf used for lei
Mai Tai	island rum drink
Makaloa	finely woven pandanus mat
Mauka	inland
Mokihana	native fragrant berry used for lei
Malihini	newcomer
Malolo	flying fish
Mana	a sensitivity or inner power
Moopuna	grandchild
Muumuu	Hawaiian shift-type dress
Naupaka	native shrub
Obi	broad sash worn with a kimono
Ohana	family
Okolehao	potent drink made from roots of ti plant
Paina	small native dinner
Pakiki	stubborn
Palaka	native checkered material
Pau	finished
Pareu	wraparound skirt
Pidgin	Pidgin English, fractured English and Hawaiian
Pikake	delicate white, fragrant blossom used for lei
Pipikaula	Hawaiian jerk beef
Poi	Hawaiian staff of life made from taro

Punee	movable couch
Puolo	lei or food wrapped in ti leaves as gift
Pupu	snack
Tabi	Japanese cloth footwear used for reef-walking
Ti	native green leaf plant
Tutu	grandma
Wana	sea urchin
Yukata	Japanese cotton material used primarily for kimonos